F
Hurd, Forence.
Secret of Canfield House

Secret of
Canfield House

Secret of Canfield House

Florence Hurd

THORNDIKE
CHIVERS

This Large Print edition is published by Thorndike Press®, Waterville, Maine USA and by BBC Audiobooks Ltd, Bath, England.

Published in 2005 in the U.S. by arrangement with Maureen Moran Agency.

Published in 2005 in the U.K. by arrangement with the author.

U.S. Hardcover 0-7862-8023-9 (Candlelight)
U.K. Hardcover 1-4056-3516-9 (Chivers Large Print)
U.K. Softcover 1-4056-3517-7 (Camden Large Print)

The text of this Large Print edition is unabridged.
Other aspects of the book may vary from the original edition.

Set in 16 pt. Plantin by Ramona Watson.

Printed in the United States on permanent paper.

British Library Cataloguing-in-Publication Data available

Library of Congress Cataloging-in-Publication Data

Hurd, Florence.
    Secret of Canfield House / by Florence Hurd.
      p. cm. — (Thorndike Press large print candlelight)
    ISBN 0-7862-8023-9 (lg. print : hc : alk. paper)
    1. Large type books. I. Title. II. Thorndike Press
large print Candlelight series.
PS3558.U532S443 2005
813'.54—dc22   2005016371

Secret of Canfield House

ONE

I am unable, even now, to see autumn foliage in all its burnt, multihued glory without a feeling of uneasiness. The sight of a child's Halloween mask, laughingly macabre, still makes me shiver. And although the color red suits my dark hair and dark eyes, I shun it. Red will always stand as a symbol of horror. It coils through my worst nightmares — when I stand again at the threshold of the white and gold room.

It didn't used to be that way.

When I was a child growing up in Vermont, fall was a miraculous season. In those days I believed in the magic of Jack Frost. His white, delicate tracks on a smoky October morning meant that he had been at work all night with his paintbrush, splashing leaves of maple, elm, and oak with indiscriminate brilliance. Halloween was a joyously anticipated holiday. I remember how we would giggle and whisper all that day at school in expectant excitement, wondering who would be transformed this year into devil, witch, or ghost.

And red. Red was just another lovely color.

But that was all long before I came to Canfield House, a house that was outwardly charming but inwardly sinister, a house that was to change my life forever.

It began, prosaically enough, the day I found myself seated in Mrs. Canfield's elegant New York apartment. I had come in answer to an ad for an "experienced, mature housekeeper." I was neither experienced nor mature, but I had kept house for an ailing father for ten years and I felt that this was qualification enough. The sad truth was (I had found through bitter experience) that I wasn't qualified for much else. In an age of automation and specialization my training had consisted of plumping up pillows, reading *Pickwick Papers* aloud, and baking custards. My humble job as file clerk had been replaced by a sleek, efficient machine, and my attempts at sales clerking and waiting on tables had ended in dismal failure.

Now, as I sat watching Mrs. Canfield adjust her reading glasses and bend her white coiffured head over my letter of application, I wondered how I was going to pay next week's rent with only one dollar and sixty-five cents. I clasped my hands nervously in my lap and sent up a silent prayer.

"Your name is Emeline Ferris," she stated in a crisp, no-nonsense way. "Miss. Never married?"

"No," I said, biting off the "ma'am." She was that kind of woman.

Mrs. Canfield went back to the letter. She was a handsome woman in her sixties, meticulously groomed, whose finely molded features were slightly marred by an occasional tic under her right eye.

"You are twenty-seven years old?" she asked.

I nodded.

"Seems strange" — her eyes, lifting over her glasses, dissected me — "that a young woman of your age would want to bury herself in the country. The job of housekeeper at Canfield House is not exacting, but the place is rather isolated and, since my son and I will be there only on an occasional weekend, rather lonely."

"I realized that from your newspaper ad," I said. I had rehearsed my little speech. "But, as I explained in my letter, I'm originally from New England. Actually, the outskirts of Dorset, Vermont. When my father died eighteen months ago,

I sold our house and thought I'd try my luck in New York. After a year here . . . I find . . . well, I find that I'm a country girl at heart and that I wasn't meant for the big city." I tried to sound casual, but there was no way I could possibly explain to Mrs. Canfield how the teeming streets of New York had become abhorrent to me. I had escaped from Dorset, small and inbred, thinking that I would find gaiety, adventure (perhaps a husband), and a new life in the city.

Instead I found a dull, dismal job, to which I scuttled each day. Here in this beehive of millions I was lonelier than I had ever been in my life. The girls at the office took me as an outlander, an alien. I did not even speak their language. Brought up as I was by a scholarly father (he had been a professor of English at Hampstead College), spending my youth between an invalid's couch and the kitchen, I had not the time or opportunity to acquire the knack for breezy small talk. When I spoke, which I seldom did, I knew that my coworkers laughed at me. "What a square!" I heard a loop-earringed girl say. "That kind of language went out with highbutton shoes."

"You have no relatives, then? No one?" Mrs. Canfield asked, eyeing my application.

"No," I said, "no one." I was thankful that for the moment Mrs. Canfield was not looking at me and did not see the rush of tears to my eyes.

Because there *had* been someone. His name was Dennis. I had met him at an office party, one of those silly alcoholic affairs where boisterous camaraderie had momentarily replaced monotonous routine. Even there, amid clamorous backslapping and handshaking, I had stood alone, clutching my punch-filled cup, smiling at no one. And suddenly *he* was there, gaily introducing himself. "Dennis is the name," he said. "And what's yours?" His eyes were hazel and green-speckled, and they radiated a glow that warmed my chill loneliness.

We went to dinner afterward. It wasn't a fancy place — just a cellar room with wine-spotted tablecloths — but to me it could have easily been "21" or the Ritz. I saw Dennis almost every day after that. He worked downstairs in the shipping department and he would wait for me each evening and walk me to my bus. Sometimes we would have dinner and sometimes we would see a movie. Dennis was going to night law school, so each moment snatched away from study or classroom was precious.

I suppose it was the old story of a young woman approaching spinsterhood, alone, unworldly, thrilled and flattered by an attractive man's attentions. But I fell in love with Dennis, or at least I thought I did. In three weeks he was talking vaguely of marriage. Of course, he would have two or three years of school, and I remember his rueful smile when he added, "Emmy, I couldn't expect you to wait that long."

The inevitable happened. I gave him my savings. Now he could quit his job and go to school full time, and we could be married. Two nights later he disappeared into the neon-flashing maw of New York. I never saw him again.

"Tell me," said Mrs. Canfield, bringing me sharply to the present, "do you know anything about antiques?"

"No, only superficially," I answered.

"I have many valuable antiques at Canfield," she said. "Some of them are fragile, irreplaceable. I would expect you to handle them carefully."

"Of course," I said. Her manner was beginning to irritate me. Did she think I would go about breaking her precious treasures?

"Also," she went on, "if you were hired, I would expect you to stay. Principally, I want a *responsible* person on the premises at all times. The two housekeepers before you were not. They left — one after a week, the other after three days — without notice. I can't abide such unwarranted behavior."

A flush of annoyance stained my cheeks. I did not care too much for Mrs. Canfield's playing the rich, testy dowager with me. This wasn't nineteenth-century New York with flocks of fresh immigrant girls eager and biddable to the most tyrannical of employers. After all, there were other jobs. But what? Spooning out corn beef hash in a steaming lunchroom? Fitting dresses on assorted fretful women? And then the sudden vision of my sunless, impersonal room facing a blank, grimy wall flashed through my mind. The thought of creeping up those malodorous stairs to it each night subdued my ragtag pride.

"I'm sure, if I'm hired, I shall stay," I said, hoping that my tone reflected some sort of dignity.

"Do you drive a car?" she asked.

"Yes. I had to drive for my father in his last years," I answered.

For a few minutes she was silent as she appraised me. It did not help my self-esteem to realize how dowdy I must have looked in my much-pressed gray wool dress compared to her fastidious attire. Her figure, heavy but trim, was outfitted in a chic beige suit, and she carried herself with straight, almost stiff-backed, poise. Finally she sighed. "Well, I guess you'll have to do."

She said it as if, having no other choice, she was indeed scraping the bottom of the barrel. A cutting retort sat on my tongue, but I suddenly recalled Father's words. "Quick temper, Emmy. That's your one bad fault. You're modest and shy enough when you aren't taking offense at someone or something. You must practice patience." How often he had said that! And how diligently I had practiced, unhappily, with not too much improvement. For now, I decided, perhaps I'd better hear Mrs. Canfield out.

"I'm pleased you can drive," Mrs. Canfield said. "That is essential, as you will be some miles from Tayburn, the closest village. Tayburn's a small place. Charming but small. You will be able to purchase food there and whatever supplies you need at Tuckerman's. We have an account. But see that you charge only those things that are necessary."

Again the barbed innuendo. I said nothing but kept my mouth tightly shut, still practicing patience.

"You will have the use of a station wagon," she went on. "You can pick it up here in the apartment's garage. It isn't a new one, but it's serviceable."

For the first time my prospective job appeared in a more promising light. I liked the idea of a car. Even though I would have the solitude I craved, I would not be marooned in isolation. And Tayburn. It sounded like one of those sleepy New England hamlets I once thought impossibly dreary but whose prospect now promised peace and quiet. My manner toward Mrs. Canfield began to soften a little.

"What is Canfield House like?" I asked.

Mrs. Canfield's stiff pose relaxed, and to my surprise she actually smiled. "The loveliest, most charming place in the world," she said. It was clear that she loved the house. "It's been in the family for almost two hundred years. The modern conveniences — electricity, plumbing, telephone — have been installed. My father saw to that. You see, Canfield House was our permanent, full-time residence in those days. In some ways my father did a rather unobtrusive, suitable job in making the place livable, but in some ways he botched terribly. Since I've recently come into a little money, I've decided to go on with

15

the restoration I began some years ago."

"Restoration?" I asked.

"Yes. Father foolishly decided that open fireplaces were passé. Those lovely old fireplaces! So he had them all boarded up and plastered over with hideous wallpaper. Awful taste that man had. I mean to have those fireplaces back. The ones on the ground floor have already been done. The workmen, after they have painted the sunroom, will start on the upstairs bedrooms. We have five bedrooms on the upper story, each with its own fireplace."

She paused and gave me a direct look. "Now, one of the reasons I want someone on the premises is to make sure that the workmen put in a full day of work for a day's pay. I find that workmen are not what they used to be in Father's time. One of your jobs is to see that they do not loiter on the job."

I nodded. Inwardly I smiled. So I was to be overseer, too. It was difficult to see myself in the role of taskmaster.

"As to the rest of your duties," she continued, "you will keep the place reasonably well dusted and polished. Mrs. Tuckerman, the grocer's wife, will come in once a week to help you with the heavy cleaning."

"And will you be coming up every weekend, Mrs. Canfield?" I asked.

"My son and I will try to make it as often as we can. I'll phone before we come. If there is to be a meal or two, I will let you know what we want. I always use the blue bedroom when I come to Canfield. It's upstairs, the front of the house. You will know it when you see it. Be sure there are clean sheets, an extra blanket, *two* pillows."

"And which of the bedrooms should I prepare for Mr. Canfield?"

"No need," she said. "When we visit Canfield House, my son prefers to stay at the Inn in Tayburn."

At the time it did not seem strange to me that Mr. Canfield should go all the way into Tayburn to spend the night when there were five bedrooms to choose from. It was only later that this oddity would come to haunt me.

"As for yourself," Mrs. Canfield said, "you may have the bedroom next to mine. It used to be the children's nursery, but I think you will find it quite adequate.

"And . . . oh, yes . . . there's Damon, gardener and handyman. Been with us for years. He's a mute, but there's nothing wrong with his hearing. He gets his instructions from me, so you won't have to be bothered with the grounds. But if you need firewood, Damon will fetch it for you." This was the simple introduction I was given to Damon, who was to be such a part of the sinister events to come.

"Damon has his own quarters in the loft above the barn," Mrs. Canfield continued. "And speaking of the barn, we use it to garage our cars. I expect you to keep the station wagon there when not in use. The night air deteriorates a car so. We take care of things, especially at Canfield."

I flushed and said nothing. Now I could see why the other housekeepers had not stayed on. Well, I reassured myself, I would only be seeing her on an occasional weekend.

Mrs. Canfield then discussed my salary, a small one but enough. Remembering how desperate my financial resources were, I was at the point of asking her for an advance. But I could not bring myself to do it. She did not seem the type that would part with a dollar unless she was sure that she would receive its worth first. So, again I held my tongue and I mentally figured how much I could borrow on an old brooch of mother's. Enough, maybe, to fill my small wants until the first paycheck.

"You may have one and a half days off a week," Mrs. Canfield said, "and you may use the car. But, of course, on personal business you are to buy your own gas."

She produced a map and gave clear, specific directions, even to landmarks, so that I would not have any difficulty in reaching Canfield House. It was situated in the south center portion of New Hampshire. The roads were good, she told me, even though the country was rugged. Only the last half-mile of road would be unpaved.

"Now," she said at last. "I think I've covered about everything. I'll want you to start at once, of course. Tomorrow morning if possible. Is there anything you'd like to know before you leave?"

I don't know why I asked the next two questions. I am not usually a person of impulse. Perhaps it was because I wanted Mrs. Canfield to know that I was, after all, human, and even though I was hired as a servant, I, too, could have an interest in the house. Or perhaps I just wanted to inject a little warmth into the icy businesslike atmosphere and leave on a note of friendliness.

"Have you just recently reopened Canfield House?" I asked.

"Yes," said Mrs. Canfield.

"And how long has it been since you have lived there?" I said, mustering my best company smile.

"Ten years," she replied coldly. The tic pulsed in her cheek. It seemed a reasonable answer to a reasonable question. And yet . . . something in the sudden freeze of her voice, the compression of her lips, her shuttered eyes, should have warned me. *This was delicate ground!* But, unlike the proverbial angels, I rushed in foolishly.

"You must have missed Canfield House in all that time," I said.

"I don't see where that concerns you, Miss Ferris," she said.

The smile died on my face.

"I hope," she said in a formal, toneless voice, "you find Canfield House measures up to your expectations. Good day, Miss Ferris." With that she turned her back.

The interview was over.

TWO

It was a crisp October morning when I started out on what was to be a strange and tragic journey. But I did not know it then as I wound the car through woodlands ablaze with color. For the first time in months I felt close to peace and contentment, reveling in the orange-golds, yellows, and reds of turning leaves as they flew past. Occasionally I would glimpse some tranquil blue lake or pond reflecting trees and sky. A stand of dark green pine would catch my eye, then a stripped blueberry patch or a group of craggy boulders. Even the bleached farmhouses standing in quiet brown meadows held a harmonious beauty.

What inviting scenes for an artist, I thought. I once dabbled in water colors in an amateurish sort of way. And although I knew I had no soaring talent, painting always absorbed me and gave me a great deal of pleasure. Perhaps I would buy some paints, a few brushes, paper, an easel and try again. Certainly my duties at Canfield House would allow for enough leisure. My mind raced on with all sorts of possibilities. Through my hobby I might even meet a kindred soul or two in the village; there might be an art class, a chance to make new friends. I needn't spend my time brooding on disappointments and disillusionments of the past.

Hope lifted my heart. The future, I knew, was a cipher, but I was starting a different life, and on that sun-drenched October day I told myself that the weeks ahead must hold some measure of happiness.

Perhaps it was well that the future was a cipher. Later I often asked myself — if I had known what was to come, would I have turned back?

I found Tayburn without difficulty. True to Mrs. Canfield's word, it was small. The main and only street consisted of a few old two-story wooden houses shaded by elms and maples: the Inn, red-bricked, bay-windowed; the post office, combined with feed store and outside gas pump; and Tuckerman's Groceries. Clearly Tayburn had not felt the tourist invasion, for there was not one "ye olde shoppe" of any kind. But it did have an air of quiet charm with its esplanade of large old shade trees, its aged, neat houses, its white church spire pointing into an azure sky.

I parked the station wagon in front of Tuckerman's. I thought I should get a few groceries before I went on to Canfield. Also, this would give me the chance to meet Mrs. Tuckerman, since she would be coming to Canfield House once a week.

It was an old-fashioned store with a wooden counter, a plank floor, and an ancient cash register. Groceries were lined neatly along shelves that reached to the ceiling. A man was behind the counter writing in a large ledger. He raised his head when I came in.

"Yes?" he asked disinterestedly. He had one of those young-old faces — he could have easily been thirty or fifty. His gray eyes were slightly protruding. His face was lined, but his hair was jet black.

"I'm Miss Ferris," I said, "the new housekeeper at Canfield."

Lantern-jawed, he said nothing.

"I think Mrs. Canfield said she would call about my coming," I continued.

"Heard you'd be here," he said finally.

"I thought I might pick up a few things before I went out to the house . . . and make your acquaintance," I ended lamely.

"Help yourself," he said and went back

23

to his ledger. I told myself that I shouldn't be annoyed at Mr. Tuckerman's unfriendliness. After all, he was only the typical taciturn New Englander, uncommunicative with any stranger, and his attitude had nothing to do with me personally. I selected several cans of soup, a can of vegetable juice, crackers, cheese, a loaf of bread. Once I turned unexpectedly and found Mr. Tuckerman gazing at me oddly. When he met my eyes, he quickly bent his head again, and his scribbling pencil was the only sound that broke the silence.

When I had collected my purchases and placed them on the counter, he said, "Want to charge them to Mrs. Canfield?"

"Yes, please," I replied.

He flipped the pages of his ledger until he found the right place. I noticed that he sported a navy blue vest with brass buttons. It seemed an eccentricity that did not quite go with his dour personality.

"I understand Mrs. Tuckerman will be helping me at the house," I said, still trying for conversation. "I was hoping I would get to meet her."

"She ain't here now," he said.

"Oh. Well, do you know what day she will be coming?" I asked.

"Next week. She goes there on Mondays," he said, as if the whole idea were distasteful.

Silence.

"Well, then," I said, a little too brightly, "I'd like to check my directions for getting to the house, just to be sure, if you don't mind."

"Don't mind."

I unfolded the map and went over the points Mrs. Canfield had specifically outlined for me. He nodded once or twice, following Mrs. Canfield's penciled-in line on the map with his finger. I noticed that the knuckles of his hands had the swollen, knobby appearance of the arthritic.

"Road's kind of rough last half-mile," was his only comment.

I refolded my map and collected my groceries. He didn't offer to help me with them. But as I turned from the counter I had the odd sensation that Mr. Tuckerman was just on the verge of telling me something. I turned my head, but he had already gone back to his ledger.

When I drove off the county macadam road onto the dirt lane that would lead me to the house, I found that Mr. Tuckerman had been right. The road was deeply gouged and rutted. Dusty clouds billowed in my wake, for it had been a dry, rainless season. But, still, there were the trees, which hung over the way like a many-colored canopy. It was almost dusk when the station wagon bounced out of the last rut, the trees parted, and I found my destination.

Canfield House was beautiful in the fading light. It was a two-story white frame house of ample, rather than large, proportions. It had freshly painted deep green shutters opening from multipaned windows. The house, squarely built in a solid, utilitarian shape, had a right wing, or "ell." I suspect that, as in many old houses, the "ell" was added in later years as the family grew. From the gray, sloping roof rose five chimneys, a large one for the main part of the house and four smaller ones for the "ell."

I drove up the circular gravel driveway and stopped at the front door with its graceful fanlight. I got out of the car and backed off to have another look at the lovely lines of the house that was going to be my new home. At that moment the last rays of the setting sun struck the windows a flaming blood red. Unaccountably my feelings of cheerful expectancy vanished. I was gripped with an incongruous foreboding. I couldn't explain it. I seemed suspended in time, my mind groping toward

26

some terrible knowledge that was important — no, vital — for me to understand. Then the sun dipped behind the trees, and the impression was gone.

I shrugged my shoulders. The day had been a long one, and I was tired. That was all. I got my luggage out of the car, unlocked the heavy door, and set my suitcases down inside the narrow front entryway.

It was not until I went back to gather my groceries from the front seat that I saw the indistinct figure of a man. He was standing at some distance, at the far corner of the house, watching me. It was getting too dark for me to see him clearly, and for a moment I was startled. I stood peering through the fading light, my arms loaded, wondering who it could be. Then I remembered. It was Damon, the gardener. I started to walk toward him, thinking that he might not have known that I was coming and hoping that I could explain. But I had only taken a few steps when he disappeared around the side of the house. Tomorrow would do for introductions, I told myself.

Tonight I was eager to explore my new home. I left my packages and my luggage in the hallway and started with the ground

27

floor. I knew little about colonial architecture, but I realized from the wide plank floors, the gleaming oaken paneling, and the low timbered ceilings that this indeed was a very old house. And though I didn't know a Chippendale from a Queen Anne, I felt that the pieces of furniture were not only exquisite but well suited to the rooms they graced.

The hallway divided two front parlors, or sitting rooms, one now obviously used as a dining room. Through the hallway (which had a half-enclosed stairway rising to the second story) and past a swinging door was the kitchen. Here was a delightful room. In spite of its large fireplace, which once must have been used for cooking, baking, and heating, the appliances would have pleased the most modern of housewives. There was an oven artfully built into one paneled wall. The burners were an unobtrusive part of the counter, and the refrigerator purred discreetly from a recess in the wall.

Ascending from the kitchen was a second narrow staircase. There was a door that led to the cellar, and another door opened into what was a combination laundry and supply room. Beyond that was a glass-enclosed sunroom, a more modern addition.

By the time I was ready to examine the second floor, which held the bedrooms, it had grown quite dark. I found the hall light switch, which flickered, then steadied into a dim glow. At the head of the stairs the two front bedrooms overlooked the driveway. One was Mrs. Canfield's blue room. Blue-garlanded paper covered the walls; on the floor lay a small hooked rug. The four-poster bed was canopied in blue and spread with a coverlet designed in blue-white daisies.

The bedroom next to it was much smaller, and the ancient, chipped hobby-horse that stood in the corner was a reminder that this had once been a nursery. This was to be my room. The bed, also a four-poster, was narrow, little bigger than a child's bed but adequate enough for my five feet three inches and one hundred and eighteen pounds. The rest of the furnishings were simple: a chest of drawers surmounted by a misty mirror, a small desk, and a rocker. A large braided rug containing all the colors of the rainbow gave the room a warm and cozy look. On one wall a sampler, done in blue and red stitching, proclaimed: *Spare the Rod, Spoil the Child.*

I went down the long hallway to look at

the other rooms. There were two huge bathrooms, old-fashioned but installed with modern plumbing. The next two bedrooms, one on either side of the bathrooms, were also large and furnished sparingly, with the usual four-posters, commode turned dresser, and braided rugs.

The last bedroom was at the back of the house. The door here, unlike the others, was tightly shut. I tried the handle and thought the door was locked. After some jiggling of the knob I found that the heavy door was only jammed, and I pushed it open. Instantly it seemed that a chill, evil wind enveloped me. Hesitating there on the threshold, I had the eerie feeling that I had left the rest of Canfield House far behind. It was not unlike the same strange sensation I had felt earlier when I saw the windows of the house reddened by the dying sun.

I grew cold and shivered. I am not a highly imaginative person; I have never given credence to superstition, the occult, ghosts, or other esoteric powers. Yet, for some unknown reason, I did not want to go into that room. All my instincts told me to slam the door and hurry back to the warm cheerfulness of the kitchen. Reason, logic, and common sense argued that I was acting foolishly. If I were to stay in this house comfortably and alone, I must not allow myself to harbor ridiculous, fearful notions on my first day.

I groped along the inner wall and found the light switch. Although the illumination here, like the downstairs hall, was dim, I could see at once that this was a very different room from the others. It was a white and gold room, alluring, feminine, and luxurious. At least twice the size of the other bedrooms, its floor was covered with thick, plush white carpeting, which sank beneath my feet. The enormous king-sized bed dominated the room. It was decked in white satin, edged with gold bands. The white wallpaper had a bold design of golden poppies, and the poppies were repeated on the shades of full-blown, gilded lamps, which squatted on the bedside tables. Fluffy crisscross curtains were held in place by gold tasseled bands.

It was a room designed as a gorgeous setting for a woman. Real enough, bright, almost brazen, it was hardly the background for what some would call "manifestations." But somehow, for all the modern beauty of the room, the irrational fear I felt on the threshold stayed with me.

31

There was an aura of unholiness that seemed to hang over this voluptuous place.

I forced myself to walk across the thick carpeting to the tri-mirrored dressing table. At once it struck me that this room, in contrast with the scrubbed cleanliness of the rest of the house, was dusty and neglected. Festoons of silvery cobwebs hung from the ceiling. The curtains were yellowed, the tasseled bands tarnished, and I'm sure that if I had stamped upon the rug, I would have raised a powdery cloud of dust.

Over everything there lingered an odd, sweet smell, faint but repellent. On the wall close to the window a strip of wallpaper had been torn away and then repasted hastily, so that the design was completely awry. It was an inconsistent flaw in the rich, though soot-covered, decor. But then I recalled Mrs. Canfield's telling me that each of the bedrooms had a sealed fireplace and that some years ago work had been begun to restore them. This had evidently been the case here.

The dressing table, filmed with dust, held several jars and perfume atomizers. Behind the row of crystal bottles was a large, framed photograph. I picked it up. The portrait, in color, was that of a beautiful young woman with gold-blonde shoulder-length hair. Her gray eyes, slightly uptilted, smiled secretly. Her mouth was full, pouting, and sensuous. The nose was finely shaped, though short. Around her slender neck was a double strand of pearls that, even in the picture, seemed to glow with a life of their own. Her face seemed so vitally alive, so provocative, so right for this white and gold milieu! The inscription carelessly scrawled at the bottom of the picture read: "To my darling, Arabella."

Arabella. Mrs. Canfield had not spoken of an Arabella. Had she been a daughter who died? But there was no family resemblance; not one feature of this face could be remotely connected with Mrs. Canfield. And I had assumed that her son, since he lived with his mother, was a bachelor.

I stared down at the photograph. The beautiful gray eyes seemed to mock me. Did I detect a touch of cruelty in their depths? Was it fantasy that this lovely face, this white and gold room, were but masks hiding some dark unknown secret? Nonsense, I told myself. Mrs. Canfield would probably have some sensible explanation. But why hadn't she mentioned the room? Most incredible of all, aside from its very existence among antique, austerely furnished rooms, was the fact that finicky Mrs. Canfield had allowed her cleaning woman to overlook it.

Standing there with the picture in my hands, I suddenly felt the muted stillness of the poppy-decked walls closing in on me. I tried to fight the feeling that the inanimate objects around me — the quilted chaise lounge, the enormous bed, the very jars on the dressing table — were watching me. The triple image of my pale, strained face, caught in the mirrors, looked back at me. With shaking hands I replaced the photograph and hurried from the room.

I made my way to the kitchen, determined to shake my uneasy mood. A cup of hot tea and some food would do the trick. I had not eaten since noon. Good, solid sustenance, I told myself, would banish my inane fears. I found the tea easily. But there wasn't much that was edible in the refrigerator. A jar of pickles, some chutney, a limp celery stalk, and some cheese was all it contained. Grateful for my foresight in stopping for groceries before I came, I fixed myself two cheese sandwiches and a cup of strong tea and brought it to the large, round kitchen table.

I was hungrier than I thought. The sandwiches soon vanished, and I debated opening a can of soup. Instead I poured myself yet another cup of tea. I was limp and exhausted; every muscle in my body ached. Yet, my mind continued to race in feverish circles around the enigma upstairs. I tried to think of practical things. Mentally I ticked off a list of tomorrow's schedule. First I must unpack my suitcases. Then I would go into Tayburn for more groceries, check the supply of clean sheets and towels, see that there was enough wood for the fireplaces, introduce myself to Damon, find out if there was sufficient oil for the furnace . . .

But it was no use. My mind constantly returned to the white and gold bedroom upstairs. I could not fathom its incongruity or its strange effect upon me. I was reminded of my father, who would say when I was frightened or apprehensive, "If you are thrown by a horse, the only way to conquer your fear is to get right back on him." We had never owned a horse; this was merely Father's allegorical way of telling me that to dispel fear one must meet it head-on. Yet, I knew that tonight, anyway, nothing in the world would induce me to go back to that room.

I was lifting my third cup of tea when a

slight noise froze my hand. Below me, in the basement, there was a muffled bang, like the slamming of a door. My heart stopped while I waited tensely for the sound to repeat itself. But there was nothing. I don't know how long I sat there, cup poised in midair, waiting. Finally I replaced the cup, rattling it against the saucer with unsteady fingers.

Had someone come in or gone out? Was there a door leading up from the basement to the outside? Perhaps it was only Damon, seeing to the furnace. But it was an oil furnace, and it wasn't likely that it needed tending — not at this time of night. *I really should go and investigate,* I argued with myself. *Mrs. Canfield had hired me as a responsible person.* Still, I made no move.

Then my straining ears caught the sound of scratching on the door that led from kitchen to basement. "Who is it?" I called in an unnaturally loud voice. The scratching came again. I tried to repeat the question, but this time the words caught in my throat. "Who . . . ?" I began hoarsely.

And then the taut, charged moment was snapped by a distinct "Meow!"

It was a cat! Only a cat. She must have gotten in through a window in the basement. I laughed out loud. The laugh was slightly tinged with hysteria, but the relief was so great I could have just as easily cried.

I opened the basement door, and there stood a large yellowish-gray tabby. She tiptoed past me into the kitchen, her tail flicking at my legs. "So it was you!" I said. She ignored me and with immense dignity padded across the floor toward the swinging door. She would have pushed herself through had I not caught her. "Not so fast," I said. She made no protest when I picked her up, but merely looked at me out of yellow, reproachful eyes. I saw that she was in the family way — in fact, motherhood seemed very imminent, and I had no doubt that she was searching for some corner in which to have her brood. I put her out the back door into the yard. Again she didn't complain but sauntered off into the night, her tail riding high.

I sighed as I watched her go. What had become of me? One day away from civilization and I had become a case of jittery nerves. It wasn't a very good beginning, and I simply had to take myself in hand. First of all, the window in the basement had to be locked if I didn't want Mrs. Tabby back. I didn't think Mrs. Canfield would appreciate a batch of new kittens nesting in her house.

Squaring my shoulders, I went to the head of the basement stairs. I found the light switch easily. It wasn't as bright a light as I would have wished, but the room it illuminated was just . . . well, just an ordinary basement. There was the oil furnace, a preserve cupboard, a discarded manual washing machine, a tub, and some stacks of newspapers neatly tied in bundles. Yes, an ordinary basement, or cellar, as we called it back home, and I kept repeating the phrase like a mindless tune, as if it were some charm against the unknown.

Nevertheless, I stepped briskly down the stairs, not daring to look into the shadowy corners. I found the window and fumbled with the rusted hook that served as a lock. As I slipped the hook into the catch my hands trembled, to my vast annoyance.

THREE

I awoke the next morning with the sun winking through the elm outside my window. Drowsily I watched a bushy-tailed squirrel scramble up one branch. Motionless on his perch, he regarded me inquisitively. Was I still asleep and dreaming? What had happened to the grimy window and blank, brick wall that usually greeted me first thing?

And then I remembered. I was at Canfield House, and the blank wall was only a bad memory. I gazed at the play of golden light upon the umber, vermilion, and yellowed leaves and thought, "How lovely!" Last night's doom-laden fears seemed ridiculous in the clear blue light of morning. The picture of mama cat and her imperial tail brought a smile to my lips. Even the back bedroom and its chilling effect receded. It had been simply the exaggeration of an overtired mind. Evil materializations, I reminded myself as I dressed, were for tales told around a crackling fire on a rainy night, or for idle, super-stitious minds. They had nothing to do with the realities of the work-a-day world and nothing to do with me. Hadn't Father once told me that I hadn't a bit of the psychic in me? I was somewhat of a romantic, a little foolish at times, he had chided, but not the kind that took to flights of ghostly fancy. Poor Father! He had tried to make a well-rounded scholar of me, his only child, but had only succeeded in turning out a well-behaved young lady who had learned her lessons by rote, who used good grammar, and who now and then dreamed of knights in shining white armor, knowing all the while that such dreams were absurd.

I went downstairs through the swinging door to the kitchen. There was some coffee in a canister, and the coffee pot was easily found. Soon the warm aroma of perking coffee filled the kitchen. I admired again the hand-hewn ceiling beams and the nut-brown paneling that had been preserved so lovingly through the years. The house, Mrs. Canfield had said, was almost two hundred years old. Had it been built during the Revolution or just after? What had the first Canfield, coming upon this site in the wilderness, been like? Stiff-backed, too, no doubt, for it would have taken immense fortitude to found a home in a rugged country in those inhospitable times. A sampler on the wall above the fireplace instructed: *Pride Goeth Before Destruction.* I could imagine some Canfield bride laboriously stitching away on this homely quotation from the Bible as a reminder to her husband that humility had its worth, too. Whatever else they had been, the Canfields had built well. Only a solid structure could have withstood two centuries of torrid summers and frigid New England winters.

Then a thought struck me. Mrs. Canfield had said that the Canfield house had been her father's. How then, I asked myself, had she come to have Canfield as her married name? Had she, like so many aristocratic New Englanders, married a distant cousin of the same name? This seemed credible, and I could imagine her great pride in being able to hand down her ancestral home to a son with the surname of Canfield.

As I was having my second cup of coffee the workmen drove up in a battered panel truck. There were two of them — energetic and vigorous, exactly to Mrs. Canfield's taste. One was a good deal older than the other, and he wore his billed painter's cap

41

set squarely down upon large, protruding ears. His cragged face had the ruddy look of robust health. The younger one so closely resembled his partner that I guessed them to be father and son. He was endowed with the same protruding ears and wore his cap pushed back on a springy thatch of brown hair.

"Pa and I are supposed to paint the sunroom today," he said, by way of introduction. He did not seem at all surprised to see me, or by the fact that there was a new housekeeper. "Mrs. Canfield picked out the color last time she was down."

"Fine," I said. "I'll help cover the furniture in there."

"No need," he said. "Pa and I can do that in a jiffy. The only thing is" — he hesitated — "well, I hate to do this to the Missus, but, you see, Pa and I, we had this here roofing job we promised a long time ago . . . and . . . we got to get at it starting tomorrow."

"Oh, but Mrs. Canfield said . . . ," I started in dismay.

"No need to worry, ma'am," he interrupted. "We'll get the other thing done just as fast as we can and then we'll be back here to start on the fireplaces, like we promised."

"When will that be?" I asked.

"Couple of weeks. Two, three."

"A couple of weeks? But Mrs. Canfield was counting on you!" I could already feel Mrs. Canfield's cold disapproval. I wasn't doing very well as work foreman right from the start. "You gave your word," I added desperately. "You promised."

"Promises don't mean much at *her* wages," the older one cut in, his face turning a deeper shade of brick. "Me and the boy has to take the promises that pay the most."

"Now, Pa, let me handle this," his son said. The father picked up his paint buckets and carried them into the sunroom. "Pa's apt to get a little excited now and then," his son went on. "Truth is, this man we're going to work for has got to get his roof on before the cold weather sets in, and he can't get no one else to help. He's up a tree, that's for sure. And he's done us lots of favors, and we can't turn our backs on him now. Can we?"

I didn't know whether or not he was telling the truth, but what difference did it make? I could see that I couldn't persuade him and his father to stay.

"Them fireplaces up there," he added, "they've been standing there for two hundred years. They'll keep. But you've got to have a roof over your head, that's for sure. Right?"

I could only agree, but I knew that Mrs. Canfield would not. I would have to call her and I dreaded it.

Putting the unpleasant off, I strolled outside to have a better look at the grounds by daylight. The sun was a warm, gilded ball by now, and its heat upon my back was pleasant. I inhaled deeply. The scent was almost heady — sharp and clean. In the distance above the line of dark firs a wisp of smoke drifted toward the sky. There were no other houses in view. I walked to the edge of the driveway. Shrubbery lined the outer and inner curves of the drive. The center circle held zinnias, now shriveled from the first frost of the year. There was a rough path that led off into thick woods, which bordered one side of Canfield House. The road on which I had arrived skirted the outer perimeter of trees. On the other side of the house a tawny meadow ran down to a small stream. The air was so still, so crystal clear, it was as if the scene had been caught on a picture calendar. For a moment I forgot Mrs. Canfield. It was the kind of miraculous day for a stroll in the woods or a ramble along the weed-lined stream.

I was tempted, but I resisted and reluctantly turned back to the house. There were things I should be doing. For one, I had left the station wagon out all night. Remembering Mrs. Canfield's caution about the car, I had a momentary twinge. I went quickly into the house to get the keys. As I was mounting the stairs I heard one of the workmen calling to me. "Say, Miss! Miss!"

I came into the kitchen. "I hate to bother you" — it was the younger one — "but we need some old newspapers if you have any. There's just a small patch of floor we haven't got covered."

"I don't know about newspapers," I said. "I . . . oh, yes! I saw a stack of old newspapers in the basement last night. Come along, and I'll show you."

Even though it was bright day outside, the basement was dim enough to require a light. I descended the stairs with the painter behind me. "They're over there in the corner," I said as we got to the bottom. Now that I was there in a calmer mood, I looked around casually. There were actually two windows, both long and narrow and grimy with dirt. The one I had locked the night before was directly opposite the stairs. The other was some distance away but along the same wall. There was only one entrance to the basement, and that led from the kitchen. A boarded-up coal chute had provided ingress at one time in the days when coal was used for heat, I supposed.

"Miss . . . ," the workman called to me. "Miss, these here papers are too old. They'd fall apart if I untied the string. I don't think I could use . . ."

But I wasn't listening. The hook of the window I had thought I had locked was undone! But I was sure . . . Had my trembling fingers not fastened it securely enough? True, the lock was rusted and insecure, but even so, no cat or other animal could have pushed it open from the outside once the hook was in place. A tingling uneasiness ran through my veins as I realized that the window, though narrow, was large enough for a man to roll through.

I jumped at the tap on my shoulder. "Lady . . ." It was the painter. "Is anything the matter?"

I swallowed hard. "No," I answered. I had not secured the hook properly. And that was all. "Nothing is the matter."

"Those newspapers," the man said, "they must have been there since the year one. I can't use them."

"I'm sorry," I said, "but I don't think there are any others. I'll see if I can find an old cloth upstairs."

I found a few rags in the utility room, and he said they would do.

I got the car keys and drove the car down the narrow drive to the back of the house. The reconverted barn was only a short distance from the house across a hard-packed back yard. No grass or shrubbery grew there, only a single gigantic oak. It was very old, its trunk gnarled and twisted, its branches spread wide. It was the sort of tree children love to climb and must have been a favorite for the Canfield offspring.

The barn was salt box in shape and newly painted white to match the house. The huge double doors were closed by a wooden bar, but there was no lock. I got out of the car and lifted the bar, then drove into the dark and musty interior.

Sunlight came in feebly through a high, narrow window. When my eyes became accustomed to the gloom, I could see that there were crude stairs leading to the loft. I got out of the car and looked around. It was a huge, cavernous place. Rusted farm machinery, giant misshapen relics, indicated that some Canfield, not too far in the past, had once grown crops. Along one wall were stalls, now empty, which had perhaps held horses or livestock. I could almost imagine the smell of hay. Curious, I started to walk over to the stalls.

It was then I heard the sound behind me. It was a soft, persistent shuffling, like something heavy being slowly dragged across the floor. I paused to listen. They were footsteps! And they were coming closer. I whirled. "Who's there?" I asked, trying to stiffen my voice with an authority I didn't feel. "Who is it?" The words echoed and reechoed among the haunting shadows.

The shuffling stopped. In the gloom I could make out the towering figure of a man. He came a few steps closer. Now I could discern a pair of dirty overalls. "Who are you?" I repeated. I tried not to show my shock. I had never seen an uglier face. The man had a harelip; his slack, jawless face was unshaven. Red-rimmed eyes stared down at me from under thick brows that met across the bridge of his nose. "What are you doing here?"

He said nothing but planted his huge bulk in front of me, blocking my way to the door. Then I could see that his hideous mouth was working soundlessly.

Damon! How stupid of me. Of course, I should have known. This was Damon, the mute gardener, the man I had seen the night before at the edge of the house.

"You're Damon," I said, smiling weakly.

He gave a slight dip of his head, but the scowl on his forehead deepened.

"I'm Miss Ferris, the new housekeeper," I said lightly, while my heart lurched against my ribs.

He nodded again.

"Maybe Mrs. Canfield hasn't had a chance to tell you. I just came last night . . . I . . . hope . . . we can get along," I added. I could think of nothing else to say.

His head dipped once more.

He could hear and understand all right; at least I hoped he could. Yet, he made no move to let me pass. His bearlike form stood solidly in my path.

"Well" — I tried again — "I . . . must . . . be getting back to the house."

His mouth moved wordlessly.

How could I made him understand? Or was it that he did understand and was trying to tell me something? If I only had paper and pencil. But what if he couldn't write?

"Is there something you would like to tell me?" I asked. All the while, I was looking wildly about for some means of getting past him and out into daylight. Although he had not made a threatening move toward me, I could sense his hostility, and it scared me.

"Can you write?" I asked.

He shook his head in the affirmative.

I needed writing materials. I had left my purse at the house, taking only the keys. And then I thought of the glove compartment in the car. Maybe I could find a pencil and a scrap of paper there.

"I have some paper and a pencil in the car," I said. "If you let me get it, you can tell me whatever it is you want me to know."

At last he stepped aside. I forced myself to walk slowly past him. An odor of stale sweat and whiskey emanated from him. I had an impulse to bolt for the door, but instead I got to the car and opened the glove compartment. Damon had followed me closely.

I found a stubby pencil and several gas receipts. The backs of the receipts were blank and, unless Damon's message was long, would be adequate.

He accepted the pencil and paper in blunt-fingered, dirty hands. Leaning against the hood of the car, he began to write. I could hear his heavy breathing as he slowly covered one small piece of paper, then another. Finally he was through and handed his message to me. It was printed in large block letters and read:

MY NAME IS DAMON. THE BARN IS MY PLACE. I DON'T WANT NO ONE HERE LOOKING AROUND.

"But I wasn't looking around," I protested. "I was just parking the car. Mrs. Canfield said that I was to keep it *here*."

He nodded and motioned for me to return the paper. Again he wrote, slowly and painfully. This time it said:

YOU WAS LOOKING AROUND TOO.

I did not know what to answer. It was true I had been on my way to inspect the stalls when he came up from behind. But how was I to know that I was intruding on Damon's private sanctuary? Suddenly I felt disgustingly annoyed with Mrs. Canfield. Why hadn't she told me that Damon resented strangers in the barn? She could have at least prepared me for him, especially since she had made such a point of keeping the car garaged here.

"I didn't mean to look around," I said finally. Damon had again assumed his menacing stance, and I found myself pressed up against the side of the car. "I'll have to park the car here, though. But that will be all." I could have promised him that after today's episode I did not care if I ever saw the inside of the barn again.

"I *really* have to get back to the house," I insisted. After an interval he finally stepped aside. But even as I walked out into the happy, sweet sunlight and up the drive toward the house, I could feel his blood-rimmed eyes upon me.

I had been at Canfield House less than twenty-four hours and had met nothing but unfriendliness, fear, and enmity. Was this a portent of things to come?

FOUR

I re-entered the house, chagrined and exasperated. My "simple" housekeeping job with its attendant benefits of leisure, country air, and relaxation was proving to be frustrating — and, though I hated to admit it, fearful. Well, I could always leave, I reassured myself. But could I? With no money and no transportation except Mrs. Canfield's car, where and how would I go? No, I had to stay — for the time being, anyway — and practice patience. I could make my departure if I wanted to and could face Mrs. Canfield's wrath after my first payday.

I went into the sunroom, where the smell of fresh paint was strong. The workmen were having an early lunch and sat with their backs against a sheet-covered divan, munching thick sandwiches. The younger one looked up when I came in.

"Have a bite?" he asked in a friendly tone. His father went on eating and ignored me.

"No, thanks," I answered. Heartened by the younger one's invitation, I thought I would make one last attempt to persuade the two of them to stay. "Would you reconsider your decision," I asked, "if Mrs. Canfield offered you more money?"

The older man snorted. "That would be the day. She'd squeeze a nickel until it squeaks."

"No, ma'am," the younger one said. "In the first place, I don't think Mrs. Canfield would pay us more than she said. And in the second place, like I told you, this other man needs his roof."

There was nothing to do but to telephone Mrs. Canfield. When a maid answered the phone and told me that Mrs. Canfield was out for the day, coward that I was, I breathed a sigh of relief at my temporary reprieve. I left a message to be called and then went upstairs to finish my unpacking.

My closet was tiny but sufficient for my skimpy wardrobe. The gray wool, a green jersey, a black "basic," two paisley prints (bought on sale at Macy's), four skirts, and three inexpensive cottons were the sum total of my hanging items. In addition, I had a few blouses and two "good" sweaters. The drawer space was limited, too, and the drawers of the ancient dresser stuck. As I yanked and pulled on the bottom one I couldn't help wondering if this was one of Mrs. Canfield's "fragile" antiques. But the drawers, once I had them opened, were permeated with such a delightful odor of lavender that I forgave the dresser for its cantankerous old age.

Later I went down to the kitchen, where I checked supplies. Clearly I wasn't expected to exist on chutney, pickles, cheese, and crackers, and I would have to go into Tayburn to stock up. Tomorrow morning would have to do for shopping. I dared not miss Mrs. Canfield's telephone call.

The workmen left at five. They had done a good job; the walls were a fresh, pale green with not one telltale splatter of paint on the dark woodwork. The furniture had been pushed back in place, and the floor thoughtfully mopped. The sunroom was a light, airy place furnished with wrought iron table and chairs. The divan was covered with a gay floral chintz, green ferns intermingled with purple lilacs. This, I supposed, was where the family had their meals during the hot summer, for it did not get the afternoon sun.

My supper was a can of soup, bread, and cheese. I was just sitting down to eat when the telephone rang. It was Mrs. Canfield. And I was right to anticipate her reaction. She fairly erupted when she heard my report. "What do you mean 'they have another commitment'? I won't hear of such a thing! Put Mr. Granowski on this minute."

"They've already gone home," I said.

"And you let them?" Her voice was cold with fury.

"It's after six," I answered.

"No sense of responsibility," she went on. "Just pick up and leave anytime they want to. I can remember when one got an honest day's work for one's money. And yes, a promise was a promise."

"They said they'd be back to work on the fireplaces in a few weeks," I ventured.

"A few weeks! The idea! They're fired. They'll never get another day's work from me. When I say I want those fireplaces done, I want them *done!*" There was an angry humming on the line. "Well, my father always did tell me when you want something done, see to it yourself."

I knew that she was referring to my inability to keep the workmen on. I was just on the point of telling her that it was not my fault that they had left when she said, "I'll have Miles drive me up tomorrow. Never mind about dinner. We'll eat at the

Inn. Just have plenty of coffee." With this she hung up.

The next day was Saturday. I made an early quick trip into Tayburn for groceries. Mr. Tuckerman waited on me in complete silence, but this time I hardly noticed. I was anxious to get back to the house in case the Canfields should come.

I needn't have hurried. The hours stretched, one by one, interminably, and still they did not arrive. To keep the minutes moving I invented all sorts of tasks. I scrubbed the stainless steel sink; I polished the pewter; and, cloth in hand, I dusted every corner, every knick-knack, twice. There was a collection of old glass on the sideboard in the dining room, which I handled with especial care. Among the lovely pieces, and the only one I could name and recognize, was an Irish cut-glass bowl. Later I was to learn that this was truly a museum piece, a genuine Waterford, with its characteristic scalloped edge, sunbursts, and horizontal prisms.

I avoided the gold and white room. Somehow, even in broad daylight, I could not force myself to enter it. It was obviously unused and omitted in the general cleaning routine, and I had no need for feeling guilty for overlooking it. Strange, I thought, that the rest of Canfield House should be so normal, even comfortable, once the door of that room was closed.

I saw Damon only once that day. I was upstairs adjusting the curtain in Mrs. Canfield's blue room when I glanced outside. Damon was cleaning out the flower bed in the center of the circular driveway. He looked up just as I parted the curtains, his face ugly and hostile. Nevertheless, I managed a watery smile and a weak hand wave. I was determined that, since I had to live close to this man, I was not going to shake in my shoes every time I saw him. If Damon noticed me, he made no sign but bent to his weeding again.

The Canfields did not arrive until long after the supper hour. She came hurrying into the front parlor where I had built a blazing fire against the October chill. It sent a warm, reflected glow on the highly polished floor and paneling. Mrs. Canfield went immediately up to the fire and held out her well-manicured hands to the warmth.

"Ah, seems as if you would have *some* sense, Miss Ferris," she said, nodding toward the fire. "It's turned quite cold outside. Oh, Miles," she called over her shoulder to the man entering the room with a blue overnight case, "just put it down anywhere for now."

He came up to the fire where I was standing with Mrs. Canfield. "This is the Miss Ferris I was telling you about, Miles," she said by way of introduction.

I found myself looking up into a pair of deep blue, magnetic eyes. "Nice to know you," I mumbled.

He studied me, his thin mouth curled into a half-smile. "How do you do, Miss Ferris," he said at last. Tall, sinewy, he carried himself with a lazy arrogance that only the self-assured possess.

"I hope you had a nice trip up," I ventured, grasping at the first banality that came into my head.

He did not reply at once but continued to study me. His chiseled features resembled his mother's. (I was soon to learn that his tongue could also be like hers, tart and tactless.)

"Nice enough," he finally said.

Mrs. Canfield had, meanwhile, seated herself on the horsehair sofa and was busily engaged searching her purse. For the moment she ignored us.

"Lovely country," I murmured. "And Canfield is a charming house."

He ran a hand through his tousled blond

hair. "Do you really think so?" he asked in mock seriousness.

"Yes . . . I . . . Canfield must have an interesting history . . . being so very old . . ." His steady gaze was making me uncomfortable.

"Old it is. But you aren't. I can see that. I thought housekeepers were supposed to be frumpy maternal types."

I did not know what to say. I felt that he was baiting me and I knew I should resent it. But there was a masculine electricity about him that was captivating, despite his sardonic smile.

"I hope you outlast the others," he said.

Now the blood rushed to my face. "Perhaps I will."

"Oh, well. You might at that," he answered, turning to the fire.

Mrs. Canfield broke in, "Come sit here, Miss Ferris. There's this business to talk over." I went over to the sofa and sat down beside her. "Now, about the workmen," she said. "I feel . . ."

"Oh, Mother," interrupted Miles in exasperation, "why you want to throw good money after bad on the old hen-roost here is beyond me."

"We've been through all that, Miles," said Mrs. Canfield. "It's *my* money, and every penny is worth it." She gazed about the room with pride.

"You just don't make sense to me sometimes. Argue over a twenty-five-cent shortchange but spend a fortune on a rattly old chair that no one would sit on, anyway," he said.

"I love old things," she said. "Besides, they're a good investment. You wouldn't understand."

"Understand? Oh, ho, yes I do. Pride, possessiveness. But at what price?" Now I could detect bitterness in his tone.

"Miles, Miles," she reproved. "Why don't you take my bag up while Miss Ferris and I have a little talk?"

He shrugged, picked up the overnight case, and carried it from the room.

"Well, Miss Ferris," said Mrs. Canfield, straightening herself, "I'm sorry that you have not been able to manage things a little better. You were here just one day and the workmen quit."

"They didn't quit, Mrs. Canfield," I said. "They simply . . ."

"They didn't have a firm hand," she interrupted. "And as far as I'm concerned, they have left my employment."

I could feel the hot blood rushing to my face. Never had I felt so much like a reprimanded schoolgirl. "Mrs. Canfield," I said, "I did the best I could. If you feel that someone else could do better, perhaps I'd better leave." Patience had come to an end.

Her eyebrows went up in faint surprise. "That won't be necessary, my dear," she said in a mollified tone. "It's done, and that's that." For Mrs. Canfield that was an apology of sorts, and being beggar rather than chooser, I accepted it.

"Miles and I have scoured the countryside this afternoon," she went on, "trying to round up someone who will be more reliable. It seems that most of the able-bodied men have gone to work in the shipyards or someplace like that in Portsmouth. It's too expensive to import anyone from New York. We'll just have to let it rest for a bit. But I'll find someone, never fear."

I was sure that she would. Mrs. Canfield (I had already learned) only accepted retreat as a temporary expedient.

"Have you had your supper, Mrs. Canfield?" I asked by way of changing the subject.

"Hours ago. At the Inn. Ah, the Inn used to be a charming place, really. But now that a few tourists have discovered it, they're talking of expanding the dining room. A pity. The Inn was actually once a tavern in colonial times, and the dining hall used to be the old tap room. Can you imagine hordes of gum-chewing rubbernecks invading that beautiful old building?"

"Come off it, Mother." It was Miles who had come downstairs again. "If it means money in their pockets, why not?"

"Money isn't everything," she answered, almost primly.

"Haaa!" he snorted. "Is that why you sold the last of the farm two years ago?"

"Oh, piffle! That was just common sense. There was no one to farm it. It was just going to waste. *You* never were interested in it, goodness knows. You don't even like the house. The minute I go and you get your hands on Canfield House, it will be up for sale."

"You bet your sweet life!"

"Miles," she said, "the past is the past . . ."

"Never mind, Mother!" he interrupted sharply. "I'm sure that Miss Ferris isn't interested in our quibbling." He stood in front of the fire, his face tense with anger.

"We're tired, my dear. It's been a long day," Mrs. Canfield said with more gentleness in her voice than I thought she was capable of having.

His face relaxed then, and he took a pipe from his pocket.

Mrs. Canfield turned to me. "Now, then, are there any problems you want to discuss while I'm here?"

"Yes," I began, hesitantly. "I'm . . . I'm afraid the gardener seems to resent me." I did not want to tell them how badly he had frightened me.

"Damon?" asked Mrs. Canfield. "Why should Damon resent you?"

"I don't know . . . it's . . . it's" — I groped — "just the way he looks at me . . . his hostile attitude."

"Hostile?" said Miles. "It's just your imagination. Damon happens to be unfortunate in his face. And he's shy because of it. Terribly shy."

Shy was not the word I would have picked to describe Damon's threatening stance in the barn.

"Oh, he's all right," said Mrs. Canfield. "He's been with us for years. I doubt whether you took the trouble to know him."

I said nothing to that. Mrs. Canfield, I felt, had already placed me in the category of inept hired help. The fact that she undoubtedly placed others there, too, served to smooth my ruffled feathers. If I could learn to ignore her acid tongue, I told myself, I could endure her infrequent visits.

"Did you find everything in order when you arrived?" asked Mrs. Canfield. "I hope so. Mrs. Tuckerman, although reliable, is sometimes a little forgetful."

"Everything was scrubbed and polished to perfection. Except . . ." I hesitated, remembering the thick layer of dust in the white and gold bedroom.

"Except what?" asked Mrs. Canfield.

"Why, the back bedroom," I answered. "The bedroom done in white carpeting. It looked like it . . . well . . ." I paused. For suddenly there was a tense and watchful silence as both mother and son stared at me. "It's the only room that seems to be . . . ah . . . neglected."

Nothing was said. I could feel the silence magnifying, expanding, and then drawing in on me. Mrs. Canfield's facial tic became more pronounced. Miles broke the silence.

"Wasn't the door locked?" he asked. I saw that his face had paled beneath its tan.

"Why, no," I answered.

"That's odd. I thought . . . ," he began.

"It doesn't matter," Mrs. Canfield broke in. "Perhaps Mrs. Tuckerman went in to give it a dusting."

"But it hadn't been dusted, or at least it didn't seem to be," I added weakly. For there was a meaningful silent exchange between mother and son.

"Well, we don't bother with *that* room," said Mrs. Canfield with a briskness that I felt was forced. "I mean to have it done over."

"I don't mean to pry, Mrs. Canfield," I said, for by now my curiosity had overcome my awe of my employer, "and I know this isn't my concern. But the room is part of the house, so naturally when I inspected the other rooms, I went into that bedroom, also. There was a photograph . . ." I should have had the good sense to stop right there, but my tongue went on as if it were an independent entity. "It was of a lovely young woman called Arabella. I wondered who . . . ?"

My unfinished words hung in the air.

Then Miles turned and angrily tapped the coals from his pipe into the fire. "Miss Ferris, must you *know* everything?" he asked with scorn. And then to his mother, "Good night! I'll be at the Inn. See you in the morning." He strode from the room. The door slammed as he went out into the night.

"We don't talk about Arabella," said Mrs. Canfield sternly. "She is Miles' wife."

FIVE

Arabella was Mrs. Miles Canfield!

For a long time after Miles had left for the Inn and Mrs. Canfield had gone up to bed, I sat watching the dying fire. I was more mystified than ever. If Arabella was Miles' wife, where was she? Were they separated? Divorced? Mrs. Canfield had spoken of her in the present tense, so she could not be dead.

"We don't talk about Arabella," Mrs. Canfield had said. I was an outsider, the housekeeper, and it was reasonable that the Canfields would not want to discuss their private affairs with me. But there had been an undercurrent of something more than just the avoidance of gossip. I recalled the exchange of significant glances between mother and son when I had mentioned her room, and the paling of Miles' face when he had said, "I thought that room was locked." Why should it be locked? And how lightly Mrs. Canfield had dismissed my mention of its unused, cobwebby state!

That Arabella's name aroused strong feeling in Miles was apparent when he had bolted from the room. Had memories of his wife something to do with his not wanting to spend even a night at Canfield House?

In the fireplace an ember sparked and glowed. It was growing cold, and I was tired. I dampened the fire and went up to my room. Before I got into bed, I stood before the dim, scrolled mirror hanging over my dresser and examined what I saw objectively. Arabella was beautiful, but what was I? My hair was not long and silky blonde, but an ordinary brown, worn parted on the side, short, just barely curled under at the ear lobes. My nose was a little too broad at the nostrils; my mouth, no matter how I smiled or tried to pout, was just an ordinary mouth. It was true that my eyes were my best feature, large and well set, but there was no provocative enchantment in their depths. The self-critical inventory did nothing but reveal what I had always known, that I was stuck with an unexciting face and that it would have to do.

It took me hours to fall asleep. When finally I did, it was to uneasy dreaming. In my dream Arabella floated into my room, her seductive figure barely concealed by a white, filmy negligee. She stood over my bed looking down at me, malicious, silent laughter in her gray, uptilted eyes. I lay there terrified, some inner voice telling me that this was only a nightmare. I wanted so desperately to get up and run from the room, yet my limbs were leaden. I could only look up at her in frozen terror.

"Why, you're plain," said Arabella, leaning over me. "Not quite homely but plain. No competition there." She laughed soundlessly.

"It's only a dream," I wanted to shout at her. "You're not real." But I had no voice, no tongue. I had become mute like Damon.

And then Miles came through the door. His handsome face was stern, his eyes blazing. He did not even glance at me. It was as if I were not there at all. "Come away, Arabella," he urged. "Come to bed."

"Make me," she said teasingly.

He grabbed her and tried to kiss her while she struggled. Her long blonde hair whipped wildly about her face as she sought to break his hold. Suddenly he let go, and before she could recover her balance, his hands went to her throat. I could see her screaming, but no sound came from her lips.

I jerked awake, wet with perspiration, my heart pounding in my ears. My eyes roved wildly about the room. Black shapes peopled the shadowy dark. Slowly my eyes picked out the dresser, the chair, the hobby horse. There was nothing more. It was some minutes before I could fully persuade myself that it had really been a dream. The night was very still. Outside my window the elm was traced in jet against a dark sky. Not a breath of air stirred its few clinging leaves.

I lay there for a long time with the aftertaste of the nightmare in my mouth. I must stop puzzling over the Canfields, I told myself; I couldn't have many more of *those* horrors. However, my resolve was futile. Again, as I closed my eyes, I envisioned Arabella floating, ghostlike, into my room. I saw her tormenting, smiling eyes and heard her cruel, thoughtless words: "You're plain." Was Arabella really as entrancing and spiteful as she had been in my dream? And how could I explain my graphic picture of Miles' savage attack upon her?

I tossed and turned, trying to push the nightmare from my mind. Clearly the Canfields and Canfield House had entered into my life in a perturbing way. What I could not see as I moved restlessly on my pillow that night was that I was to become a part, although small, of a tragedy that had begun years ago and was even now unfolding its final and ultimate act.

Finally, toward dawn, I fell into a deep sleep.

I awoke to the sound of my name. It was Mrs. Canfield, and she was shouting. "Miss Ferris! Miss Ferris! Are you up?"

The small traveling clock on my bedside table said nine-thirty. I sprang out of bed with alarm. "Yes," I called. "I'm up."

"I'd like some coffee, please. And hurry!" Her voice carried imperiously.

"Coming!" I shouted as I flew into my clothes.

I stopped at her bedroom, knocked, and went in. She was propped up in bed, her white hair still perfectly coiffed, as if she hadn't slept at all.

"I'm . . . sorry . . . ," I began.

"Overslept?" she asked. She was wearing her reading glasses, and there was a book spread out on her lap.

"I'm sorry," I repeated. "I . . . I had a bad night."

"Rubbish! What on earth could *you* have a bad night about? You're too young to be troubled by ghosts."

I stared at her in silence. Ghosts? But

71

there had been no ghosts. It had only been a dream.

"Oh, for goodness sake!" she said. "Stop gawking. I'd appreciate a cup of coffee as soon as you have it made."

I flushed, an angry retort on my lips. But she had returned to her book. I swallowed my annoyance and satisfied my temper by slamming the door as I left.

Later, after I had taken Mrs. Canfield her coffee and returned to the snug kitchen, I poured a cup for myself. Looking out at the beautiful morning, with the blue, autumnal haze just beginning to lift and the sparkling sunshine dancing on the great oak's branches, my irritation with Mrs. Canfield and even the horror of my nightmare began to fade.

Miles came for his mother at eleven. They were planning to drive to an auction near Keene. "Never know what you can turn up at these auctions," said Mrs. Canfield. "Why, I bought that good Hepplewhite chair from a farmer in Connecticut last year. For a song, too." It was hard to tell whether it was the Hepplewhite chair or the "song" she had paid that gave Mrs. Canfield her air of satisfaction.

"Come along, Mother," said Miles. Declining my offer of a cup of coffee, he stood impatiently in the hall, waiting for Mrs. Canfield. In the daylight I could see he had fine lines around his eyes and the beginning of a furrow over the bridge of his nose. He gave me the benefit of his sardonic smile. "Nice weather," he said. "Good country air, Miss Ferris."

I was conscious of my uncombed hair and my pale lips. This morning, I supposed, I was closer to Miles' idea of "frumpy" housekeeper. But why should I fret over *his* opinion?

"Yes, isn't it?" I replied, in what I hoped was a flippant tone.

"I'm ready," said Mrs. Canfield, drawing on her gloves. She turned to me. "I'll keep in touch with you, Miss Ferris. Mrs. Tuckerman will be here tomorrow morning. See that she polishes the silver this time."

And with that they both went out into the October sunshine.

Mrs. Tuckerman came promptly at eight-thirty the next morning. I saw her through the kitchen window as she descended from a vintage Ford. She was the most enormous woman I had ever seen. Not in height, for she was shorter than I, but in bulk. She was one round dumpling from the tips of her toes to her several quivering chins. And crowning this portly aspect was a shock of amazing orange hair. On top of this rode a tiny black straw hat stuck through with a pearl hatpin.

"You're the new housekeeper," she said breathlessly as I let her in the kitchen door. "I'm Dolly. Dolly Tuckerman, but Dolly to you." She held out a small dimpled hand. Like a good many stout women, she had a pretty, sweet face, smooth-skinned and radiant with health.

"I'm Emeline Ferris," I answered.

"Well, I'll call you Miss Emmy, if you don't mind," she smiled.

"No, of course not." I had warmed to her already. She was the first person who seemed human since I had come to Canfield House.

She removed her hat carefully. "I had a cousin by the name of Emmy," she said conversationally. "She was a real fine person." She put the hat into a cupboard. "Oh, Mr. T. said he'd met you the other day."

"Yes . . . I stopped for groceries." I remembered how word-bound the storekeeper had been and what a contrast his wife was.

"A bit close-mouthed," she said, as if

reading my thoughts. "Mr. T. isn't one for conversation. But he's a good man. Comes of a good line, too. They used to be sea captains back in the old days, the Tuckermans. That's *really* what Mr. T. would like to do. Go to sea. But the shipping business died out long before Mr. T. was born. He's resigned to it. Wears his vest with the anchor buttons and goes down to Portsmouth now and then to watch the ships come in. But he's happy to come back home to Tayburn."

"Would you like a cup of coffee before you start?" I asked.

"Not now," she said. She produced a large apron from a paper bag she had brought. The apron was designed with huge, outsized roses, and when she tied it on, she looked rounder than before. Somehow, I could not help but wonder how a woman of her girth could be agile enough for the cleaning of a two-story house. But she moved easily and lightly. "I like to get in a few licks before I take my coffee break," she said. "You go ahead and have one if you want. While I'm polishing up the ovens and cleaning the refrigerator you can sit here and have a cup, and we can get acquainted."

"Can I help?" I asked.

"Not with this," she said as she removed a rack from the oven. "You can give me a hand with the dusting when I get to the other rooms."

When she said "dust," I suddenly remembered the white and gold bedroom. "Everything is so well kept up except" — I hesitated — ". . . the back bedroom. It looks like it hasn't been cleaned in a long time."

Dolly turned from the sink, where she had been scrubbing the oven racks. She regarded me with her round, liquid brown eyes. "That room is supposed to be locked."

"Well, it wasn't last Thursday," I said.

"Now, can you be sure?" she asked.

"I was in it," I said.

Her face grew thoughtful for a moment. "The housekeeper before you — Mrs. Donovan, I think, was her name — could have carried the key off by mistake. She *was* a harebrain. Lasted only three days." Dolly gave a short laugh and shook her head. "She'd jump if you'd say 'boo.' "

"Mrs. Canfield thought that you might have gone into that room to clean it," I said.

"Me?" she asked incredulously. *"Me* go in that room? First place, I've got plenty of

other things to do. Second place, that room gives me the willies. I don't know why, but I don't like to go in there. Maybe just because it reminds me of unhappy times. Or maybe . . . well . . . because there's just something about it."

So, matter-of-fact, light-chattering Dolly had felt it, too. The cold evil that hung over the rich, expensive furnishings was not just part of a delusion.

"I told Mrs. Canfield that I'd work here and work hard. But in *that* room, no!"

Knowing Mrs. Canfield's penchant for a "day's wages for a day's work," I wondered how she had let Dolly have her way.

"Mrs. Canfield didn't object?" I asked.

"No. She said it wasn't going to be used, anyway. She didn't press me about it. Besides, it ain't easy to get good help out here in the country. And I been with the family since when they lived here before."

"But what is there about that room?" I asked, half to myself.

"I don't know," said Dolly. "I don't believe in ghosts or hauntings myself. Besides," she added, "Mrs. Miles ain't dead."

"You mean Arabella?" I asked.

She nodded.

"But where is Arabella?"

"*She* didn't tell you much, I expect,"

said Dolly. "They don't like to talk about it. Not that I'm a gossip, you understand, but I don't see how it hurts to know a few things about the family you're working for." She dried her hands and poured herself a cup of coffee. She loaded it with cream and sugar, then sat down at the table opposite me.

"Well, about twelve years ago," she began, "Mrs. Canfield and her son were living in this house. That is, Mrs. Canfield stayed all the time, and Mr. Miles came up weekends. He worked in New York. Still does. Something like insurance, I think."

"What about Mrs. Canfield's husband?" I asked.

"Oh, Mr. Canfield, he died years ago. When Miles was just a little thing. Mrs. Canfield brought the boy up herself. You can be sure he's the apple of *her* eye. Only one she doesn't boss around."

"No, he didn't strike me as a mother's boy," I said.

"He takes after his Ma, that's why. He's got a will of his own. Not that he isn't fond of her, mind you, but he does pretty much what he pleases." She took a sip of coffee. "Well, one weekend — Miles was about twenty-five, I think, at the time — without

78

so much as a by-your-leave he brought Arabella home to Canfield House as his bride."

"Hadn't he told his mother he was going to get married?"

"No. Knew his mother wouldn't approve. And he was right. She was madder than a wet hen. First place, Miles hadn't consulted *her*. Second place, Arabella West didn't belong to the upper crust. Mrs. Canfield was angling for Mr. Miles to marry one of them society debs, but I guess the first minute he laid eyes on Miss Arabella, that was it. And she was gorgeous. Can't say I blamed him."

I felt a small twinge, remembering my dream and how in it Arabella had pronounced me plain.

"Where did he meet her?" I asked.

"She was a secretary down at the place he worked. Her Pa, I heard, had been just a plain factory worker. But Arabella got herself educated and landed this job, and then Mr. Miles."

Dolly drained her cup. She went on. "Oh, Mrs. Canfield gave him a going over, I can tell you. In them days I was working a couple days a week here, and I happened to be in the kitchen that first morning after he brought her home. I could hear them all the way from the parlor, going at it hammer and tongs."

"Were they happy?" I asked. "I mean, Miles and the new Mrs. Canfield?"

"Oh, Mr. Miles was. Just wild about her. The first thing he did was redo the back bedroom the way she wanted. Even if they did come up just for weekends. All that white carpeting and them gold tassels. Mrs. Canfield was fit to be tied all over again when Mr. Miles had her precious floor planking covered. 'Looks like one of those bawdy houses,' I heard her say. And he fired right back, 'And how would you know, Mother?' I guess Mrs. Canfield could have put her foot down real hard because it is *her* house, at least until she dies. But she was afraid that if she did, Mr. Miles wouldn't be coming weekends anymore, so she let it pass. But she simmered. That she did. She always spoke of it as 'that awful room.' "

"And did Mr. Canfield and his wife keep coming up every weekend?" I asked.

"Oh, yes. Mr. Miles was fond of his mother, for all her bluster. And he liked it here. That is, in *them* days he did."

"And Arabella?"

"Oh, she, *she* hated it. Stayed in her room mostly, doing her nails and fussing with her hair. They'd go out to the Inn for dinner, and once in a while they'd bring friends from New York, but mostly they'd come alone. She'd come into the store on Saturday morning for a magazine or nail polish, her lovely face pouting. 'Beats me,' she'd say, 'why anyone would want to bury themselves before their time in a place like this.' "

"But where is she now?" I asked, my curiosity goading me on. "Where did she go?"

"Well," said Dolly, carrying her empty cup to the sink, "that's another long story. She ran off with another man. I'll tell you about *that* sometime, but if I don't get at them floors, Mrs. Canfield will give me what-for."

I felt guilty for having detained her, ashamed that I had been so intrigued about something that was clearly none of my business. Dolly bustled about getting mop and waxer. "Isn't there something I can do?" I asked, wanting to make up for the time she had spent talking to me. And then I remembered Mrs. Canfield's instructions about the silver.

"Mrs. Canfield wanted the silver polished," I said. "I could easily do that. You have so much else to do."

"That's sweet of you, Miss Emmy," she said. "The silver's in the dining room sideboard. Lovely pieces. Hardly gets used now, though. 'Twas about the only thing that Arabella didn't take."

"Oh?"

"Cleaned Mr. Miles out, she did. Took all the money and every one of those expensive trinkets he gave her. He would have given her the moon, too, and maybe she'd have taken that!" Dolly said this without malice, but she shook her chins sadly. "You know, the terrible part of it is that I think Mr. Miles still cares."

Did he? I wondered. Did Miles still care for Arabella? And what if he did, I scoffed inwardly. Why should it matter to me? Inconceivably, it did.

SIX

The next morning I drove into Tayburn. My first stop was at the post office, since Mrs. Canfield had indicated she might send me a note through the week. I knew there would be no personal letters. I had long since stopped my correspondence with the few friends I had in Vermont. Their early mail had filled me with shame, asking so eagerly for news of my successes, the exciting places I had been, the people I had met. How could I tell them that I had had only failure, that I had eaten in cellar restaurants, hardly exciting, and that the only person I had met had humiliated and deserted me? My encounter with Dennis had only strengthened my desire to cut the past from my life.

Dennis! How many hours I had spent brooding over his betrayal. I had tortured myself with such self-recrimination; certain that the scar of my unhappy encounter would last forever. And yet, I suddenly realized, in the past few days I hadn't thought of him once. So much for a broken heart! I was going to live without his bitter memory. I knew that now, and the knowledge was a healing balm to my wounded pride.

The Tayburn post office was a small cubbyhole in one corner of the feed and supply store. The plaque at the barred window announced: "Postmistress Haney."

"Is there anything for the Canfields this morning?" I asked of the woman who was busily sorting mail. "I'm Miss Ferris, their housekeeper."

She looked up. "Oh, so you're the new housekeeper."

"Yes," I answered.

The postmistress was a white-haired, elderly lady who might have been anybody's grandmother except for the lighted cigarette between her meager lips. She wore her gray-white streaked hair pulled tight from her face in a pincushion bun. Beady eyes sparked from behind rimless glasses. She was dressed in a navy blue cotton housedress, which hung loosely on her small, sparse figure.

"Miss Ferris," she repeated, squinting through a veil of smoke. She turned and, standing on tiptoe (I noticed she wore bedroom slippers), rummaged through a bank of pigeonholed shelves. "There's just this today," she said without removing her cigarette. She handed me a postcard, leaning forward so that her face was only inches from the barred window. "How are things up at Canfield House?" she asked.

"Just fine," I answered.

A long ash fell from her cigarette, but she ignored it. With an eagerness she did not attempt to disguise she asked, "They all getting along O.K.?"

"Just fine," I repeated.

"Seems like things have been awful quiet up there lately," she continued conversationally. Her voice had an unpleasant, grating quality.

"Why shouldn't they be?" I said.

"Well, I can remember when they wasn't. You know them Canfields, they . . ."

"I must be going," I interrupted. "Thank you, Mrs. Haney." I left her with her face peering out from behind the window, a wisp of smoke trailing after me. I was sure my reluctance to chat must have been a great disappointment to her.

The postcard was from Mrs. Canfield. She had forgotten to give Damon instructions to clip the driveway shrubbery; also, I was to purchase a new pair of clipping shears. Would I do that? The purchase of the shears was easy; it was facing Damon and trying to communicate with him that would be difficult. I had seen very little of him since our first encounter, and I didn't look forward to the next.

From the post office I crossed the street to Tuckerman's. Dolly was there behind the counter, and she gave me her dimpled smile as I came in. "Why, good morning, Miss Emmy. Lovely day, isn't it?"

"Working in the store today?" I asked.

"Oh, I give Mr. T. a hand now and then," she said. Mr. Tuckerman was in the far corner, busily stacking canned goods. He ignored my presence.

"What will you have on this wonderful day?" she asked. Her brown eyes twinkled.

"I guess I'd better get some . . . ," I began. I pawed through my oversized handbag for the list I had compiled that morning. "I've forgotten my list. I was sure . . ."

"Never mind," said Dolly brightly. She waved a plump arm. "Just look around. You might remember. Groceries, dry goods . . ."

"Dry goods," I said. "Have you any aprons? Seems I only brought two, and I'd like another one."

"Sure," she said. "Let's try the dry goods department, then."

She came from behind the counter and steered me over to the shelves that contained tea towels, washcloths, undershirts, and aprons. On the shelf next to the aprons were assorted paper hats in orange and black and a stack of Halloween masks.

"Oh, I'd forgotten!" I exclaimed. "It's almost Halloween."

"Halloween's today, Miss Emmy, *today!*" she said with almost childish excitement. I knew that the Tuckermans had no children of their own, but I imagined that Dolly, with her sweet nature, would love youngsters, and their holiday time would be hers, too. "The kids are having a big party at the school tonight," she went on, "and I always help my neighbor, Mrs. Sawyer — she's got five — fix their costumes. Last year we got the oldest, Benny, up as a walking paper bag of groceries. He won first prize, too. You should have seen him . . ."

"Bunch of nonsense!" It was Mr. Tuckerman. He glared at us over a pyramid of canned applesauce. "Halloween's just an excuse for the kids to go wild."

"Now, Mr. T.," admonished Dolly, "you was probably the biggest cutup of them all when you was little."

Somehow, I could not imagine Mr. Tuckerman as ever having been little.

"We was well-behaved in them days," he mumbled, and went back to stocking supplies.

"He's not a bad sort," whispered Dolly. "He don't really mean to be short. Poor Mr. T.'s had some disappointments the last few years. Turn any man a little sour. Lost his savings in a bad investment; then his arthritis come on right after." She shook her head. "But, still, he's a good man," she said. "It's just his way."

With Dolly's help I managed to recall the rest of the things I needed. She toted up the charges very neatly in the ledger and put my purchases in two large brown paper sacks.

"Oh, yes," I suddenly recalled, "I'll need a pair of clipping shears."

"You can get those in the feed store," said Dolly. "Are they for Damon?"

"Yes," I answered. And then I added, "Have you known Damon long?"

"Heavens, yes," she said. "Ever since he was knee-high. Poor thing!"

I looked at her quizzically, for it was hard to think of Damon's scowling visage and dirty overalled bulk as "poor thing."

"Ah, well, the kids used to make fun of him," she explained. "Wasn't his fault he had a harelip."

"Was he always mute?"

She shook her head. "No. When he was a child, some rowdies, out for a lark, dumped him in Tayburn Pond and left him. Forgot, or didn't know, that he couldn't swim. Mr. Miles just happened along when poor Damon was going under. Jumped right in and dragged Damon out. Mr. Miles was just a boy himself, maybe two, three years older than Damon. Ever since then Damon hasn't been able to speak."

"Is he . . . I mean . . . is he all right otherwise?" I asked.

"Oh, he's not mental, if that's what you mean. Not real bright, but certainly not backward."

"But he seemed so . . . so unfriendly." That was the only way I could express myself.

"Just his way, Miss Emmy. He's shy and wary of strangers. He wouldn't hurt a flea."

I was beginning to realize that Dolly was one of those kindly souls who wouldn't speak ill of the devil. So I was not too reassured in her assessment of Damon.

"Why, he's so devoted to Mr. Miles," Dolly continued. "Follows him around like a puppy. Mr. Miles has had him as a gardener for fifteen years. Fixed him a nice room in the stable loft, with plumbing and all. He's as cozy as a bug in a rug up there."

"And the others . . . I mean . . ."

"Oh, he's loyal to Mrs. Canfield, too. After all, she *is* Mr. Miles' mother. And Mrs. Canfield don't have too many complaints. He stayed on the place all those years they were gone. He's kept the grounds up fine all these years, and there ain't many who'll go out there and work for as cheap." She paused for a moment, and a slight frown creased her smooth forehead. "He never did like Miss Arabella, though. And she couldn't abide him."

"But why? He never comes in the house. I don't see how Arabella would care one way or another about Damon," I said.

"I heard she tried to get Damon fired," said Dolly.

"Fired?"

"I expect Damon knew too much."

"Too much about what?" I asked.

"Well . . ."

"Dolly!" It was Mr. Tuckerman. He came over to us and his white, stony face was suffused a deep red. "You know I don't hold with this gossip-mongering. Just go about your business like you're supposed to. And forget all this jibber-jabber about the Canfields."

"Now, Mr. T.," said Dolly, unperturbed by her husband's outburst, "we was just having a little chat."

I hurriedly picked up my paper sacks. I didn't want to be the cause of a family quarrel. "It's all right. I was just going," I said. "I'm sorry to have taken up so much of your time. Thank you, Dolly. I'll see you next Monday."

"Good-bye, Miss Emmy."

Mr. Tuckerman's stony disapproval followed me out the door.

I made a quick stop at the feed store, picked up the shears, and then started toward home. As I drove through brown, sere countryside my thoughts again were of the Canfields. I was thinking of mother and son, and how Arabella must have affected their lives. I could well imagine Mrs. Canfield's resentment of her glamorous daughter-in-law. Although she did not seem overly possessive of Miles, as were most widowed mothers who had brought up an only son, it must have pained her that he had chosen a girl with an unacceptable social background. Mrs. Canfield, with her inbred sense of thrift, must have been appalled at Miles' showering of expensive, lavish gifts on his bride. And then the crowning insult, of course, would have been the white and gold bedroom, a desecration of Mrs. Canfield's carefully preserved Canfield House.

And Miles himself. If Dolly was right, how passionately in love he must have been with Arabella, and how horribly wounded his male pride when she ran off with another man. Yet, I mused, that was ten years ago. In ten years, surely, the wound should have healed. (Mine had in a few days!) But even now the mention of her name was something he could not bear. "He still cares," Dolly had said. Did he? I asked myself again.

What part did Damon play in all this, Damon who "wouldn't hurt a flea"? How did Damon come to clash with Arabella? Was Dolly right when she said of Damon, "I expect he knew too much"? Too much about what? Did he know that Arabella was going to run off with another man? And if so, loyal as he was to Miles, why didn't he communicate this information to him? Had Arabella threatened Damon? But, then, I could hardly imagine anyone threatening burly, red-eyed Damon.

When I got back to the house, I fixed

lunch — a quick sandwich and a glass of milk. Afterward I went outside to look for Damon. I hadn't seen him on the way in and I assumed he was in his loft room. So, I drove the car into the eerie half-light of the barn. Despite Dolly's reassurances that Damon was harmless, my eyes darted nervously over the phantom-shadowed stalls, expecting any moment to have his unwieldy form materialize in front of me. "Damon!" I shouted. "Damon!"

Angry with myself for being so easily cowed, I got out of the car and marched to the foot of the stairs that led up to the loft. "Damon!" I shouted again. I would come back again if he was not there, for I had no intention of going up to look for him.

Above, a door opened. Damon frowned down upon me.

"Mrs. Canfield wants you to trim the shrubbery," I called up. "And I have some new shears for you."

He shuffled slowly down the stairs. My first instinct was to leave the shears on the bottom step and run. But I was determined not to show him that I was afraid. And yet, when he finally descended and I handed him the package that contained the shears, my hand trembled. "Mrs. Canfield wants you to trim the boxwood," I repeated. Again the stale odor of whiskey and sweat reached me as he stood there dumbly. "That . . . was all," I said. He took the shears and blinked his reddened eyes. I made no pretense at further conversation but turned on my heels and left, with a dignity I did not feel. Damon, at best, as Dolly would say, "Gave me the willies."

I spent the rest of the day polishing the old pewter pots that hung from the sitting room fireplace. By suppertime, I was pleasantly tired. After a simple meal of omelet and salad I built a fire on the kitchen hearth. I had selected a book from the sitting room shelves, something like *Tayburn and its History.*

It was unbelievably dull. More like a genealogical catalog than a history, it dwelt almost exclusively with marriages, births, and deaths. My eyelids grew heavy as I tried to follow the Hunts, the Ordways, and the Canfields, and their numerous offspring.

I must have finally dozed off because I remember awakening abruptly. The *History* had slid from my lap and fallen to the floor. Sleepily I was bending to pick it up when I heard a soft tapping at the windows. Still bending over, I turned my head. The sight of the horror peering in at me jolted me upright, a scream tearing from my throat.

Even now I dream about that face. It was a sick shade of green with a gruesome, hooked nose pressed against the pane. It had crimson eyes, and its huge mouth was distended into a toothless grin. I screamed again, and the face disappeared.

By then I was fully awake, my heart clamoring in my ears. I stood up on rubbery legs. Never since I had arrived at Canfield House was I so conscious of my aloneness or of the solitary wilderness surrounding me. I could scream until my lungs burst, and who would hear? Terrified, my hypnotic gaze riveted to the windows, I waited for the face to reappear. I do not know how long I stood there. But the windows remained blankly empty, reflecting only the stainless steel sink beneath them. Gradually reason returned.

And then I remembered. Halloween! Hadn't Dolly told me that this was All Hallow's Eve? I smiled in relief. Some child or children, I told myself, had come by for trick or treat. Since I had been asleep and not heard a knock at the door, he or they had gone tapping at the window. And my ridiculous screaming had scared whoever it was away.

I did not dwell on the slight improbability of children coming to Canfield

House, so far from town, or its nearest neighbor. Instead, I reassured myself by thinking that perhaps in an area where trick-and-treat pickings were lean, children would be more apt to wander farther afield.

Halloween and the simple explanation of the green face at the windows notwithstanding, I locked every door and window, and barricaded my door with a slat-backed chair. The chair, I realized, was not much of a barrier, but its presence under the knob helped give me some sense of security.

I did not sleep well that night. As soon as it was daylight, I got up and dressed. I ran down the stairs and, without stopping to put water on for coffee, I went out the back door of the kitchen. During the night a disturbing thought had come to me about the Halloween episode. It seemed to me that the kitchen windows, from the outside, were too high for any but a tall man to reach.

And I was right. The top of my head was about two feet from the sill.

But, I reasoned, clutching for a rational explanation, if it had been a small prankster, couldn't he (or she) have stood on a box or a stump of wood? However, there was nothing in front of the windows but a dripping water tap. A child could not have reached the windows to look in by balancing on the water tap unless he had the agility of a monkey. I looked about for a discarded box or crate. The hard-packed yard lay innocently empty under the spreading oak.

The sun was rising now, an immense, crimson globe in a purple and gold streaked sky. Its first rays gilded the roof of the barn. Ordinarily I would have watched with delight the changing sky and the spreading light. Now I could only shiver with chill apprehension.

There *had* to be a reasonable answer. Perhaps one child had boosted another upon his shoulders. I turned back to the ground beneath the windows, where the water tap had made the soil soft and muddy. This time I did notice something. In the damp earth were two footprints. They were large footprints. By no stretch of the imagination could they be considered as belonging to a child. The footprints were distinctly ribbed, as if made by rubber-soled sneakers. Staring down at them, cold with fear and anger, I knew who had made them.

Damon wore sneakers.

SEVEN

I don't remember eating breakfast that morning. But I do recall washing up the breakfast dishes and dropping a cup from my nerveless fingers. It shattered into a dozen pieces. I stared at the broken shards at my feet, wondering vaguely whether the cup had been "good" china or not. The thought that Mrs. Canfield would reprimand me for breakage, whether the cup was valuable or not, helped to steady me.

As I swept up the broken china I told myself that for my own peace of mind I must have it out with Damon. I would *not* have him frightening me. He had no reason for his hostile attitude. He must be made to understand that I would not put up with childish tricks. I was here to stay at Canfield House, whether he liked it or not. And I would tell him so at once.

I stamped out of the house and down the path to the barn. But when I got to the double doors, my determination vanished. I could clearly visualize myself lecturing to

Damon's whiskey-dimmed eyes, his mute, shapeless mouth. What would I say? "You must stop scaring me" or "Why don't you like me?" What good would it do, when I had difficulty communicating with him on the simplest of matters?

And, yet, I did not want a recurrence of last night's face at the window. Should I complain to Mrs. Canfield? She would only put down my fear of Damon as part of my general ineptness. And if I were to go to Miles Canfield, he would only sneer.

Then I thought of Dolly. She knew Damon well. She would know how to reach him. Perhaps she could explain my resentment of his unreasonable attitude.

I decided to drive into Tayburn immediately. I went back into the house, hastily slipped into my coat, and grabbed my purse. I would have to go into the barn to get the station wagon, but that couldn't be helped. Somehow, the prospect of meeting Damon face to face was more frightening now than ever. I scurried down the path and threw open the double doors of the barn. With racing heart I steeled myself to walk toward the car. Halfway there I heard a sound, a familiar soft shuffling. It came from the area of the darkened stalls. Throwing pride to the winds, I ran the rest of the way and tore the car door open. It took only a moment to thrust the key into the ignition and back the car out of the barn. In my rear-view mirror, through a cloud of dust, I saw Damon's ungainly form standing just inside the double doors.

Mr. Tuckerman, in his nautical vest, was sweeping the steps when I rolled up to the store.

"Early, ain't you," was his laconic greeting.

"I'd like to see Dolly," I said, trying to keep the urgency out of my voice.

"What for?" He eyed my untidy hair, my crookedly buttoned coat.

"It's about . . . curtains . . . the kitchen curtains. I want to see about having them washed." I lied. It was the first thing I could think of, for I knew I couldn't ever explain my fright of Damon to Mr. Tuckerman.

His bulging eyes studied me a moment; then he shrugged his shoulders and flicked his broom at the bottom step. "She's back of the store," he said, "in the kitchen."

I found Dolly baking bread. Her plump arms were elbow-high in flour, her pretty face flushed with the heat of the oven.

"Why, Miss Emmy," she said in pleasant

surprise, "just in time for the first loaf. Come, take your coat off and sit down."

The kitchen was an old-fashioned one, large, high-ceilinged, with an awkward, large iron range. But it was a cheerful one, too. The sun beamed through paned windows upon a yellow canary twittering and swinging in his cage above the bow-windowed seat. There were potted ferns, African violets, and two rubber plants arranged along the sills. Against the far wall, on a long, high sideboard, a blue willow teapot pouted among dainty cups and saucers.

As I sat there delighting in the warm yeasty smell of baking bread and Dolly's shining rosy face, as she punched at the dough, Canfield House and its terror seemed remote and unreal.

"What is it?" asked Dolly, studying me closely. "Now, now, I know there's *something.* You're put together all wrong this morning."

"It's Damon," I blurted out.

"Damon?" Dolly arched her finely drawn brows.

I nodded. "He . . . resents me. He's . . . well, I think he's trying to scare me."

"Why, Miss Emmy, I can't believe that. Damon wouldn't hurt a . . ."

"I know," I interrupted rudely, "he wouldn't hurt a flea." I regretted my abruptness immediately, for Dolly flushed a bright red. "I'm sorry, Dolly," I said. "But Damon just doesn't seem to like *me*."

"Whatever gave you that idea?" asked Dolly.

I told her what had happened the night before. When I had finished, she threw her head back and laughed. Great peals of merriment rolled from her, and her whole body shook like the proverbial bowl of jelly. "Oh . . . oh . . . Miss Emmy," she gasped. And then she went off again into another storm of laughter. Finally she dabbed her eyes with the hem of her apron and found her voice.

"Those children, what will they think of next?" she said. "Why, Miss Emmy, I'm surprised. Why should you think it was Damon? Damon put on a *mask* to scare you? Lord knows, he's ugly enough!"

I admitted that her statement was logical. "But those footprints," I insisted. "How do you explain those man-sized footprints?"

"Haven't you ever dressed up in your folks' clothes for Halloween?" she asked. "Old coat, old hat, old shoes?"

"Yes, but how did a child reach the window?"

"Lots of explanations for that. He could have used stilts. Carried a box and taken it with him. More likely some other friend or friends gave him a lift up."

"There was only *one* pair of footprints," I said.

"Are you sure? Maybe if you looked around, you'd find more. Or maybe only one pair stepped in the mud."

I shook my head dubiously.

"Come, now, Miss Emmy," said Dolly soothingly, "you're a bundle of nerves. Being out there all by yourself. Not seeing anyone but Damon. It would be enough to get anyone's imagination working over-time."

"It's *not* my imagination," I snapped. "Oh, Dolly, I'm sorry," I amended quickly, "but I just . . . well, I *know* I saw that face."

"Well, don't you brood over it." She patted my hand. "Let's have another cup of coffee and a slice of the best bread in Tayburn."

With the light step so characteristic of her she walked to the stove and brought the coffee and a loaf of new bread to the table. "Tell you what," she said, slicing two thick pieces from the loaf, "I think that you ought to have a dog."

"A dog?" I asked.

"Mmmm. It'll be a companion," she assured me. "You need one. All by yourself out there."

"But Mrs. Canfield would never allow it," I countered.

"I don't think she'd mind." She brought out the butter and a squat jar of homemade jam. "Long as you kept it out of doors. Tell you what — you could call and ask her."

"I don't know . . ."

"Sure you do." She placed a blue willow saucer with a slice of bread in front of me. "There's nothing like a dog for a friend. He'd be a watchdog, too. You'd feel safer."

"But where would I get one? Even if I could keep it?"

She pursed her lips while she lavishly buttered and jammed her bread. "Why," she said, her face brightening, "you could borrow Orpheus."

"Orpheus?"

"Yes. He's a mutt but a good watchdog. He looks fierce enough. Sounds it, too. But he's a sweet fellow to those he gets to know."

"He's your dog?"

"Yes, but we have two others. I think Orpheus and you would get along grand."

"I wouldn't want to take your dog," I protested.

"Now, Miss Emmy. Truth is, Mr. T.'s been complaining that we've got too many animals as it is. What with the canary, the three dogs, four cats . . . and let's see . . . there's Skinner . . . he's a squirrel . . ." She shook her head. "No, you could borrow Orpheus, and we'd hardly miss him."

Her kindness touched me. For I knew how childless women of Dolly's sort attached themselves to pets. It was really as if she were offering me the loan of one of her children.

"Dolly, that's sweet of you," I said, "but . . ."

"No buts," she said firmly. "You take Orpheus. I know you'll treat him right."

I thought of returning to the loneliness of Canfield House. A dog *would* comfort me, would give me a sense of security through the solitary dream-haunted nights. I liked dogs. When I was growing up, I was never without some kind of mixed breed (invariably called "Duke") tagging along behind me. If Mrs. Canfield did not object, why not accept Dolly's generous offer?

"I'd have to ask Mrs. Canfield before I could make a decision," I finally said.

Dolly smiled. "There's nothing like the

present when you want to do something, I say. You can call Mrs. Canfield right now. There's the phone in the store." She rose from her chair. "You go right in and call her. Do it now, Miss Emmy. You can call collect if you want. It will save you going all the way back to the house and then coming again for the dog if she says 'Yes.' "

With practical but gentle determination she steered me into the store and showed me the wall phone. I put in a call to Mrs. Canfield's apartment. It took a few minutes, and finally a male voice answered at the other end. "Who is it?" he said.

It was Miles.

"This is Miss Ferris," I replied.

"Miss . . . who?" he queried blankly. Had he forgotten already?

"Miss Ferris, the housekeeper at Canfield," I answered brusquely.

"Ahhhh, yes," he said. "And what can I do for you, *Miss* Ferris?"

"May I speak to your mother, please?" I asked.

"I'm sorry, but Mother isn't here. She won't be in until this evening."

"Well . . . I . . ."

"Could *I* help you, Miss Ferris?" I could imagine his mocking smile.

"I wondered if she'd mind my keeping a dog at the house," I said.

"A dog? Things that lonesome?" There was amusement in his voice.

"It isn't a question of that," I protested. How could he be so provoking? "I felt that I needed a watchdog."

"A watchdog? Whatever for? I can't think of a safer place than Canfield House. No danger of being robbed, mugged . . . or even raped."

I was glad he couldn't see how my face had reddened with exasperated indignation. "I suspect there might be a prowler on the grounds." I enunciated deliberately.

"A prowler? Good heavens, woman, what would a prowler be doing in that neck of the woods?"

"What does it matter?" I could not contain my anger. "Do you or don't you think your mother would allow me to have a dog?"

There was a slight pause. Then, "Ah, so you *are* made of flesh and blood, Miss Ferris. And a temper, too."

"I didn't ask for a character analysis," I said. "I'd better call back later and talk to your mother."

Miles laughed. "Don't get your back up, Miss Ferris. Sure, go ahead and get your

dog. Mother won't care as long as you
don't bring it in the house. Or anywhere
near her precious antiques."

"You're quite sure?"

"Oh, yes. If mother grumbles, I'll take
the blame."

"Very well, then. Thank you, Mr. Canfield." Without waiting for his good-bye, I
hung up. I knew that my ears were flaming.
My embarrassment was increased by the
knowledge that Mr. Tuckerman, now behind the counter and working over his
ledger, had heard every word of the conversation. I did not look at him as I went
back to the kitchen.

"Mrs. Canfield was not at home," I said
to Dolly, "but Mr. Canfield has given his
permission."

"That's good enough," she said. "Come
on out back, and I'll introduce you to Orpheus."

Orpheus was coal black except for a
patch of white under his nose that spread
across his breast like a bib. He was as big
as a police dog, but his shaggy coat indicated some collie ancestry. Although he
looked wicked enough, his long tail
wagged ecstatically as Dolly spoke to him.

I made friends with Orpheus at once. I
had always had what Father called "a way

with animals." It was only the males of the human species, I thought bitterly as Orpheus' black head nuzzled my hand, who were recalcitrant and evasive.

Dolly saw me to the car. She gave me instructions on Orpheus' feeding and handed me several cans of dog food and a length of clothesline. "Tie Orpheus up when you get to the house," she said. "He might take a notion to come back home." I opened the car door, and Orpheus sprang to the rear seat, panting expectantly.

"Thank you again, Dolly," I said.

"Take care," she beamed. She threw a kiss to Orpheus and waved as we drove off.

In front of the Inn a woman in a heavy blue sweater was burning a pile of dead leaves. The acrid smell brought back memories of other autumns when I was growing up. How I loved the foreshortened afternoons when, on the way home from school, we dug for "leftover potatoes" on Kylie's farm and then roasted them over fires in the cold purple dusk. I sighed. Now I could well believe Dolly's explanation of last night's face at the window. I had forgotten what it was like to be roaming free on Halloween night. And how could I blame any child or children for not resisting a lonely house with a lighted kitchen window? How they must have laughed at my silly screaming!

But even if it had not been Damon at the window, the fact remained that he found my presence unwelcome. Maybe, as Dolly had said, he was shy of strangers, shy to the point of sullen resentment. It was true that our encounters had either been accidental, or I had sought him out. He had made no overt move, nothing that I could put my finger on. There was no proof that he disliked me to the point of violence. I shook my head. Possibly Dolly was right. My imagination was working overtime, at least where Damon was concerned.

What I needed, I thought, was diversion, something that would take up the hours. I thought of my earlier resolve to resume my painting. Why not hunt up an art store and start right away?

Since there was no art supply center in Tayburn, I decided to drive to Darwin, a town about forty miles away. (I would, of course, keep track of the mileage and repay Mrs. Canfield for the gas used on a "personal" errand.) I had passed Darwin on the way up from New York, and it seemed large enough to have a wide variety of shopping.

I was right. I found a small book and art

store without any trouble. Then, since the day was lovely, and I was not in a hurry to get back, I had lunch at a small teashop. Afterward I strolled through the town square with its inevitable old cannon, its greened-over statue of some long-forgotten soldier of Revolutionary times, its wooden benches spaced about a clipped lawn.

In the late afternoon I drove back to Canfield House. Damon was clipping the boxwood hedge along the driveway and did not look up as I passed him. I parked the car in the back yard and unloaded my packages. Orpheus jumped out and would have wandered off on an exploratory tour, but I called him, and he came at once. When my hands were free, I would tie him up.

Before I went into the house, I could not resist examining the ground beneath the kitchen windows to see if there had been other footprints, as Dolly had suggested. To my amazement, not only were there no other prints, but the original ones were gone! There was only the lumpy dampness of earth and slight drip-drip of the water tap. I bent closer. Someone had taken a trowel or a stick and worked up the soil, so that every vestige of the ribbed sole print was gone. Damon? But why? Nothing grew along this narrow strip of ground.

Puzzled, I turned toward the kitchen door. It was then that I noticed that the door was slightly ajar. Hadn't I closed it in my hasty departure this morning? Yes, I was sure I had. In fact, I had slammed it shut. But had I locked it? I couldn't remember.

Clasping my packages, I went up the three worn, wooden steps. I noticed a clot of mud on the threshold. It looked as if someone had scraped his shoes clean before going into the house. Had I muddy shoes this morning? I was sure I had not. And even if I had, I was certain that I wouldn't scrape mud on the door sill. It was my runaway imagination, I told myself as I walked into the kitchen. I mustn't start to build false, frightening assumptions from a mere lump of mud.

I plunked my packages down on the kitchen table. My purse teetered on the edge and then fell to the floor, scattering a lipstick, my comb, and some small change. Irritated, I got down on my hands and knees to retrieve these odds and ends, which had rolled about everywhere. As I was picking up a fifty-cent piece and two pennies I suddenly froze. There were two faint, dirty footprints on the highly polished floor leading to the kitchen staircase! *They were not mine.*

Slowly I got to my feet. It seemed then as I stood in that quiet kitchen with only the sound of the tick-tocking of the pendulum clock, that the whole house was breathing, listening, waiting. I found my voice, a funny little thing I hardly recognized. "Hello!" I called. "Is anybody here?"

The empty question rebounded from the paneled walls. The echo seemed to mock me. "Is anybody here? Is anybody here?" Yet, I *knew* there was someone in the house. I squeezed the coins I had picked from the floor with icy fingers. Who could have come into the house while I was gone? It certainly wasn't Damon. He was outside clipping the hedge.

I felt a warm tongue licking my fingers. It was Orpheus. He had nosed open the door and followed me in.

His presence was a small comfort, no matter what Mrs. Canfield would say about having a dog in the house. With Orpheus at my heels, I pushed the swinging kitchen door that led into the front part of the house. Together we went from room to room on the ground floor. There were no other footprints, no muddy signs of anyone's presence.

Then, as if some invisible thread were drawing me, I ascended the steep, narrow stairs to the upper story, Orpheus following behind. I gave the blue room, my room, and the other bedrooms a perfunctory glance. I cannot say why, but I knew with uncanny certainty that whatever or whoever had intruded was waiting in the white and gold bedroom.

With Orpheus trotting at my side, fear now at the marrow of my bones, my feet moved down the hallway as if they had a separate will of their own. I thought my heart would burst with its wild hammering when I stopped before the door of that room. Finally I nerved myself to turn the knob.

The door was locked!

EIGHT

I twisted the knob again and again. The door wouldn't open. Suddenly Orpheus began to bark. Black hair bristling, ears alert, he pawed at the threshold. Panic seized me then, and I ran blindly down the hall, Orpheus bounding after me.

I tore down the stairs, out into the last rays of the dying sun, and only came to my senses when the cold evening air hit my face. Damon was still bent over the hedge. His figure loomed large and substantial in the gathering gloom. For the first time since I had come to Canfield House, the sight of him was welcome.

I ran up to him. "Damon . . . ?" I said, trying to hide my breathlessness. "Damon, I think . . . I think there is a . . . a burglar . . . upstairs." How sane and simple "burglar" sounded in place of my nameless fear!

He stepped over the hedge.

Damon's slack mouth opened; a tiny dribble of saliva clung to his malformed, unshaven chin. Had he understood?

"There's someone in the back bedroom," I repeated. I hadn't *seen* anyone, but there wasn't the slightest doubt in my mind that someone had stood behind that door while I worked so frantically to open it. "The door is locked . . . and I saw footprints in the kitchen . . ."

"Please come back to the house with me," I urged. "Please come and see." And then in my distraught state I did what I would have once thought impossible. I took his arm.

He grasped my meaning then and nodded.

Orpheus still at my heels, we climbed the stairs, Damon coming slowly behind. We came to the door. I was calmer now. Again I turned the knob.

The door swung open easily!

But it had been locked, my mind protested. I was conscious of Damon's heavy breathing and Orpheus' panting. I switched on the light and probed the corners of the room with anxious eyes. It was just as I had first seen it in all its dusty white and golden glory. There was no one there.

I clenched my fists, so that my nails bit into the palms of my hands. I went in. I looked at the inside keyhole. There was no key in the lock. Forcing myself across the thick carpet, I flung the closet doors open. There were only half a dozen empty hangers and a yellow terry cloth robe. There were no other places in that room to hide. But I got down on my hands and knees at the side of the king-sized bed and lifted the hem of the gold-banded spread. Only large gray puffs of lint greeted my frightened gaze. Nothing had been disturbed on the dressing table. There were no footprints on the rug. There wasn't one telltale sign that anyone had been there.

Finally I turned toward the door. Damon and Orpheus stood on the threshold as I had left them. Damon had Orpheus by the scruff of the neck, although the dog had not tried to follow me into the room. He stood obediently and waited, whimpering every once in a while. It was Damon who was acting strangely. His bloodshot eyes rotated warily around the room. Occasionally his tongue would dart out and lick his shapeless mouth. Sweat beaded his forehead.

Why, Damon's afraid! I thought. Damon is afraid of this room, too. He shifted his feet uneasily, and I could feel his anxious impatience to be gone.

I said nothing more about the locked

door as we went down the stairs. I thanked Damon. He grunted and scuttled through the front door.

It was pitch dark when I finally fed Orpheus and tied him up in the yard. I had no appetite myself. The chop and the salad I had fixed for supper sat barely touched on my plate. I pushed my food absently about with a fork, conscious of the shadows crowding about me. The kitchen, which I had thought so charming, was no longer a cozy and cheerful place. The clock whose ticking had seemed a comfortable sound now set my teeth on edge with its relentless counting of the seconds.

A brief scurrying behind the cellar door brought my heart to my throat. My body tensed, listening. There it was again. A scampering of . . . ? Why, of course. Mice! The house was probably plagued with mice. What old house wasn't? I had seen the traps in the pantry and in the utility closet.

I poured myself a cup of scalding tea. *This has got to stop,* I told myself. Either I leave Canfield House or I try to pull myself together. I had known that it would be lonely before I came. This tensing at every sound, jumping at every shadow, would never do. If I could only *talk* to someone sensible and practical. I thought of Dolly and her blithe, chattery outlook. Should I call her? But what would I say? Would I tell her that a door had been locked that hadn't been locked before? A door without a key? And would I discuss the footprints on the kitchen floor? Footprints that I couldn't prove were not mine? She would only laugh, and rightly so. Halloween masks and footprints! No, I couldn't ever make her understand how in some subtle way this house was working a kind of black magic on my mind, where every tiny incident sent me stampeding with alarm. I had never been afraid of lonely places. Goodness knows, with Father a helpless invalid, living as we did at some distance from the nearest neighbor, I had never had qualms about noises or shadows. And if I were to keep my equilibrium, I would push my fears aside. That is what I told myself as I sat in the Canfield kitchen, determined to be sensible if not brave. What I did not know was that terror has a mind of its own; and reason, logic, even shame of being a coward shrivel before the heat of its terrible, uncontrollable flame.

I was putting the tea away when I heard the crunch of gravel as a car pulled up to the front of the house. I went to the front door.

It was Miles.

"Good evening, Miss Ferris," he said with a satanic grin. I must have stood there looking utterly foolish, my mouth slightly agape, for he quickly added, "It's really me, Miles Canfield in the flesh. Were you expecting some other handsome young man?"

"I wasn't expecting . . . I . . . ," I stammered. "When I spoke to you this morning, you didn't mention anything . . . about coming to Canfield."

"Well, here I am. Aren't you going to let me in?" he asked smoothly.

I realized that I had been blocking the entryway. "Why . . . yes . . ."

He followed me into the sitting room, where I switched on a lamp. I was suddenly conscious of the run in my stocking (a result of crawling about the kitchen floor earlier). I knew that my face, naturally pale, was bereft of lipstick, and that my skirt was crumpled. Why didn't he phone before he came? I thought irrationally. And then, almost at once, I scolded myself for thinking that even with lipstick, whole stockings, and a smooth skirt I could possibly mean anything to Miles Canfield.

"Sorry to startle you," Miles was saying. He had thrown himself into a chair, his long legs flung out before him. Light and shadow etched his features into strong, handsome planes. "I had business in Darwin this afternoon. I flew up with a friend. We hired a plane out of New York, but he won't be leaving until early to-morrow morning. So, I decided that, since I was so close, I'd come by and see about this 'prowler' of yours. I've rented a car . . . it's only forty miles, you know. And here I am." His blue eyes smiled up at me. He pulled a pipe from his pocket and, after several tries, lit it. Because it seemed that he was about to throw his spent matches on the floor, I darted over with an ashtray.

"The perfect housekeeper," he said as he placed it on a table beside him. "But I wish you'd quit flitting around. Sit down and tell me your story."

I sat down on a straight-backed chair opposite him. "I want you to know from the first, Mr. Canfield," I said in a steady voice, "that I am not an overly, shall I say, imaginative woman?"

"Oh, I should hope not," he said. The ironic twist he gave to all his remarks rankled. His male magnetism, reflected in sardonic smile and questioning eyes, increased my irritation. I was attracted to this man. And I felt that he knew it and was amused.

"Like what?"

I told him about the face at the window on Halloween night, adding that it may have been a child's prank, but because of the high window and the footprints, I had doubted that.

"I don't see why you would think it anything else," he said. "Who would want to scare you?"

I didn't answer that because I couldn't. I had convinced myself that it hadn't been Damon, and even if I hadn't, Miles would only scoff at the suspicion, as Dolly had done. Instead I went on to tell him about the locked door.

When I had finished, his eyes still held amused detachment. "Are you *sure* the door was locked?" he asked.

"Yes, definitely locked," I asserted.

"Couldn't it have been jammed tightly shut?"

"No, I'm sure it wasn't," I said.

"Come now, Miss Ferris. You yourself admit that you were frightened. Footprints, faces at the window. You come home and find the door open, a lump of mud on the sill. Muddy shoes have traversed your kitchen floor. Before you get upstairs, you're pretty well scared . . ."

"No," I interrupted, "that's not quite true." (But wasn't it? I asked myself.)

"And furthermore," he went on, ignoring my interruption, "I have no doubt that the local gossips have embellished this place with a small air of mystery. That adds to your fright. By the time you try the door handle, you're pretty close to panic. It's quite possible in your haste you jammed the door . . ."

"No, no. I tell you . . . ," I protested. I could feel the hot blood rushing up from neck to face. He was making me seem such a fool!

"Just examine the facts," he said calmly. He looked thoughtfully at his pipe. "Tell me, Miss Ferris, are you superstitious?"

"No. Most certainly not," I replied.

"Ah," he said, "but we all have a little of the primeval fear. Especially we New Englanders. Don't forget that at one time we took to witch hanging with zest. Yes, we're still not too sure. Witches, ghosts . . ."

"I don't see what that's got to do with it," I said. "I didn't say anything about a *ghost* locking that door." I had the satisfaction of seeing the smile disappear from his eyes. I went on. "I took it for granted that some thief had come while I was gone."

"But why wouldn't a burglar go for the family silver or those glass thing-a-bobs that Mother's paid a ransom for? Why, in heaven's name, would he go up and *lock* himself in a bedroom?" He paused. "A bedroom that has *nothing*, nothing at all. Why?"

I shook my head. "I just don't know."

"Well," he said, "if it will help soothe those female jitters, I'll go up and have a look."

"Yes," I said, "I'd feel better if you did."

He pushed himself out of the chair. He went over to the fireplace and knocked the tobacco from his pipe. Did his movements seem a little slow, a little reluctant?

"All right," he said with deliberation. "I'll go, then."

He was gone a long time. Or did it seem long because I waited so eagerly for his return? What was there about this man, aside from his physical attractiveness, that I found so compelling? Oh, you stupid fool, I told myself. Miles has no more interest in you than in a bug on a stick. I must not let myself care for a man who did not care for me. No, not after Dennis. Not ever again.

Finally I could hear his footsteps on the stairs. When he came into the room, his caustic smile was gone. I thought he looked a little pale in the lamplight. His voice, however, had lost none of its scorn. "As I thought, Miss Ferris, no one has been in that room. No one at all." Then, speaking to himself, he added, "There never was."

There was no bitterness in that last statement. Just a sad emptiness. I almost felt sorry for him as he stood gazing into the cold, empty fireplace. Was he thinking of Arabella? Had that room awakened memories of happier times? They say that a man forgets more quickly than a woman. Was Miles still yearning for his golden wife? It was hard to believe that beneath his tough cynicism he had a heart that felt pain.

"Thank you," I said, breaking the uncomfortable silence. "Thank you for stopping by . . ."

He started when I spoke. "Ah, yes, Miss Ferris," he said as if waking from a dream. He squared his shoulders and came toward me. His deep blue eyes surveyed me with the old mockery. "I've made my inspection. There has been no intruder. You can go to bed safely tonight without peering into the closets or under the beds."

Any pity I had felt for him vanished. Why did he make me feel so much the rabbity spinster? "I don't make a habit of 'peering' into closets," I said coldly. "But thank you for your trouble, anyway."

He smiled then and patted me on the shoulder. "Now, I know this place could make anyone touchy," he said in a conciliatory tone, "but don't let it get to you. Actually Mother, for all her pose of *grande dame,* really does appreciate your being here. Although why she doesn't get rid of this house once and for all, I don't know. At the least, it must be a bore for you, stuck way out here in the country."

"But it isn't," I protested. Strangely enough, at that moment I felt that I could grow to like Canfield House (except for *that* room). Maybe it was Miles' presence, but suddenly my fears seemed small and inconsequential. The house was charming and comfortable. And I liked being my own master, especially after years of being at Father's beck and call. Even Mrs. Canfield's demanding ways, in the light of Miles' claim that she appreciated me, seemed trivial.

"Good," said Miles. "Then that's settled. I must say" — he scrutinized my face — "the country air agrees with you. You don't look as pale and washed out as you did when you first came." And with that backhanded compliment he left.

I went up to bed pondering over a Miles who could be a kind human one moment and a hateful devil the next. Was it bitterness over his unhappy marriage or an inherent Canfield trait that gave such caustic nuances to his speech? And yet, I told myself, what did it matter what he said? Why should I be so affected at his hurtful banter? Why should I care?

But I did care. That was the baffling thing. In spite of myself, I cared.

Long after I was in bed, I tossed and turned in the darkness, unable to sleep. One moment I felt hot, and the blankets were heavy; the next, I shivered and felt cold. Finally I got out of bed to close the window. Just as I had my hands on the sill something outside on the edge of the woods caught my eye. I stared into the dark patch of trees that loomed against a darker sky. There it was again! A tiny brief glow, like some immense firefly. It came and went several times, never moving, always at the same spot.

Was someone trying to set a fire? The woods were tinder, as was the browned-over meadow, since it had been an especially dry fall. A spark could easily set the trees into a roaring blaze. The tiny glow came again. I waited breathlessly. The glow did not reappear. There was no burst of flames, no sign of fire. What was it, then?

Suddenly it came to me. Someone, sitting or standing on the edge of the woods, had lit a cigarette or a pipe. It couldn't have been Damon, for Damon did not smoke. My "imaginary" prowler had returned. And he was watching the house!

Down below, Orpheus began to bark.

NINE

Orpheus' loud baying filled the moonless night. It was a fierce, warning clamor; but I knew that the dog was useless tied to the tree. And I could not bring myself to go out into the darkness and untie him. I wondered if Damon would hear the dog and investigate. But I supposed not. Once in his hayloft after a hard day's work, assisted, I was sure, by a generous pull or two at his whiskey bottle, he would sleep soundly.

I don't know how long I stood at the side of the window, motionless and shivering. Who was sitting out there in the blackness watching, waiting? And why? What did they want of Canfield House?

Whatever it was, I was sure it had something to do with the white and gold bedroom. But what? There *had* been someone behind that locked door today. I was certain of that. It would have been easy for him (or her) to slip out and down the back stairs without being seen when I had gone to fetch Damon.

129

Yet, my mind reasoned, wasn't it possible that I was overdramatizing, as Miles had bluntly suggested? Couldn't a passing tramp, an itinerant worker on the move, have seen the lonely house, with the occupants gone, and been tempted to enter and search for what he could find? I had caught him in the white and gold room. He had jammed the lock, and when I ran for Damon, he had made his escape. It was logical. Nevertheless, why would he be watching the house *now?*

Finally I grew too stiff and weary to think. Orpheus had long since stopped his barking. Whoever it had been at the wood's edge was gone. I crawled painfully into bed and slept deeply for the rest of the night.

The next morning, taking Orpheus with me, I inspected the spot under the trees where I had seen the glow. The tangled bayberry and the crisp brown leaves underfoot gave no sign of anyone's having been there. I looked up at my window across the hedges and the gravel drive, and tried to calculate the angle from window to woods. I moved slightly to the left and began my search again.

I was rewarded at once. There at the foot of a birch stump, nestling on some yellowed maple leaves, were three spent matches and a tiny pile of ashes. They were tobacco ashes, the kind found in a pipe. If I had had the instincts of a lady Sherlock Holmes, I would have carefully lifted the ashes onto a tissue and preserved them as a clue. A clue for what? I suppose, I thought ruefully, it would have been a clue to show that I was not losing my mind. Strange things had happened here, little unexplained oddities; yet all of them were things *I* alone had seen and could not prove.

If I preserved the ashes, then what? Who could I connect with the smoking of a pipe? Miles was the only person I knew who smoked a pipe. But that was preposterous. Why should Miles want to watch his own house?

I kicked the ashes aside with my foot. A tramp, I told myself, passing through the woods had paused to light a pipe, and I was constructing a detective novel. But inwardly I did not believe my rationalization. I was just whistling in the dark. A cold, hard knot, like an undigested peach pit, sat in my stomach.

In the meanwhile Orpheus had wandered off. I called to him, but he did not come. When I went further into the woods looking for him, I stumbled upon an old, unused road. It may have been a former logging road long out of use, for it was deeply rutted and covered with a thick carpet of leaves. I followed it for a while. Then the road dipped into a shallow brook (the same, I guessed, that came out below the meadow) and continued on the other side. I paused at the edge of the brook. There on the muddy lip were the distinct imprints of tires. They were fresh tracks, I was sure. Someone had obviously driven along that road recently.

What of it? I asked myself. Couldn't this rough road, secluded as it was, be a favorite spot for a lover's lane? What was happening to me? Must I read sinister meanings into everything?

I turned from the brook and started back to the house. Orpheus, trotting from tree to tree, soon caught up with me.

Although it was a cold November day, the sun shone unseasonably bright, and I decided that this was as good a time as any to bring out my paints and attempt a picture. I carried my easel down across the meadow to where the stream, a very tiny trickle now, whispered over the rounded stones. I set the easel up facing the woods. By now most of the trees had lost their foliage, but there was still a sprinkling of crimsons, golds, and oranges clinging to the blackened branches. Here and there a splash of green pine contrasted with the silvered trunks of birches.

It was pleasant in the meadow, with the scent of dead grasses, the cry of a distant owl, the murmur of insects. I was soon absorbed in my work. I hadn't painted for years, and although I have little talent, I had forgotten what real pleasure the creative process gave me.

Orpheus came down once, his black tail waving in and out among the high, weedy growth. He padded up to me and laid his head in my lap while I absently scratched his ears. Content at this show of affection, he trotted down to the brook, and I could hear him lapping thirstily. It made me happy to think that Orpheus had become part of me and his new home so quickly. He wandered back, sniffed curiously at my easel, then disappeared in the direction of the woods. I did not think he would wander far, so I did not bother to call him.

I worked steadily, absorbed in colors, perspective, and composition. At one time I thought I heard a low whistle across the meadow. I looked up, saw no one, and, shrugging, went back to my work. It may have been Damon calling to Orpheus.

It was past noon when I packed up my things and started toward the house. My picture was a little fuzzy and amateurish, but I had caught the colors well, and the depiction was good. I was elated with a sense of accomplishment. Not once in that long, sun-filtered morning had I given a thought to Canfield House and its mysteries.

My feeling of well-being was brief, for when I turned the corner of the house, I heard the agonizing sounds of an animal in pain. It was Orpheus. He was stretched across the bottom step leading to the kitchen door, his black, furry body convulsed and retching.

I threw my easel down and ran up to him. His eyes were glazed over, but there seemed to be a piteous plea in their black depths. I knew the signs immediately. Once I had had a Dalmatian bitch who had died in the same way.

Orpheus had been poisoned.

I did not know by what or how badly, but I had to get him to a veterinarian if I was to save him. I rushed into the kitchen and leafed through the phone book. There was no vet in Tayburn. The closest one was a Dr. Pickering in Darwin. With trembling fingers I dialed his number.

A woman answered.

"Is Dr. Pickering there?" I asked.

"No, I'm sorry he's not in. This is Mrs. Pickering. Can I help you?" Her voice had a slow nasal twang.

"When will he be back? My dog . . . I think he's been poisoned. I must see the doctor right away."

"The doctor won't be back until late this afternoon," she said. "There's a calving over to the Burnhams . . . and the Osbornes' horse . . ."

"Are you sure I can't reach him?" I interrupted impatiently.

"Yes, I'm sure. I don't expect him until suppertime," she replied.

"Is there anyone else I can call — *anyone?*" I pleaded.

"Well, now . . . ," she began placidly.

"It's urgent!" What was the matter with her?

"You say you think he was poisoned?"

"Yes!"

"Well, probably wouldn't be much use seeing a vet. If he's real bad. Sometimes they get into stuff that's set out for rats. And if it's *that* . . . well, he'd be gone before you got halfway here."

"But isn't there *someone* I could call?" I

wasn't giving up that easily.

"There's . . . let me see . . . Dr. Rich. He's sort of retired, but you might try him. His number is . . . I have it right here . . . somewhere . . ." There was an unbearable pause, during which I could hear the rustle of papers. Finally she gave me the number, and I hung up.

I did not dial Dr. Rich's number at once. I poked my head out of the kitchen door to see how Orpheus was doing. He lay stiffly inert on the bottom step. I didn't have to look closer to know that he was dead.

I covered my face with my hands. I had known Orpheus little more than twenty-four hours, but he had been such an affectionate, trusting creature that I had loved him almost at once. Somehow, I felt responsible for his death. I did not even want to think of how I would break the news to Dolly. It had all happened so fast! One moment he had been sniffing about my ankles, and the next, dead. What had he eaten? How had he gotten into poison?

I went in search of Damon. He was just inside the barn door tinkering with a power mower. The tabby cat, whom I had encountered before, played at his feet. He did not look up until I was directly in front of him.

"Damon," I said, "the dog I brought yesterday — the black dog has been poisoned."

His bloodshot eyes stared at me uncomprehendingly. Again there was the strong odor of liquor about him.

"The dog," I repeated, "is dead."

He bent his head slightly, his shapeless mouth moving.

"Don't you understand?" I was close to shouting. "The *dog* — come, I'll show you." I motioned for him to follow.

We went back to the house, Damon shuffling at my heels. When he saw Orpheus, a rasping moan came from his throat. He squatted down to examine the lifeless dog. He shook his head.

"Do you think he got into some rat poison?" I asked.

Again the blank stare.

"Rat poison," I repeated. "Poison . . ." Oh, how could I explain?

"Doesn't the barn" — I pointed in its direction — "have rats?"

He got slowly to his feet. A look of understanding unknotted his forehead. He shook his head in the negative.

"Every barn has rats," I said, still doubtful if he got my meaning.

But he shook his head again. He raised

137

his hand toward the barn. At its partly opened entrance I could see mama cat disappear into the building.

I knew what Damon was trying to tell me. He did not use rat poison. He didn't have to. He had the cat.

Even then it did not occur to me that Orpheus had been deliberately killed. It was only after I called Dolly that I began to speculate on Orpheus' death. Dolly cried unashamedly when I told her the news.

"You don't know how sorry I am," I told her. "I feel if I hadn't taken him, he'd still be alive."

"You mustn't blame yourself, Miss Emmy," she said tearfully. "But who would want to poison poor Orpheus?"

Who?

In my mind's eye I saw the flicker and glow in the quiet darkness of the night. I heard the barking of a dog. And I wondered.

"He was really such a friendly soul," she went on. "He only looked mean."

I recalled the whistling I had heard when I had been painting in the meadow. Had that been for Orpheus? But why?

"Please ask Damon to bury Orpheus." Dolly's voice broke. "He deserves a decent burial, even if he was just a dog."

"Yes, I'll do that, Dolly," I promised.

"I'd come by, but I can't get away now. Mr. T. needs me in the store," she said.

"I understand, Dolly," I said. "I'll take care of it."

For a long time after I had spoken to Dolly, I sat over the inanimate phone. People poison dogs, I thought, because they either dislike them or are afraid of them, or sometimes because the animal is a hateful nuisance. Had Orpheus been a hateful nuisance? Had the watcher in the woods wanted to get into the house and Orpheus been in the way?

Now all the little things that had puzzled and frightened me since I had come to Canfield House began to take on a deeper significance. There was no use in brushing away footprints, faces, locked doors, and a murdered dog as routine occurrences embellished by a timid imagination. It was plain to me now that someone wanted to get into the house. What was there inside Canfield House that drew this determination?

So far I had been frightened but not harmed. But what if I were in the way, like Orpheus? What then? Was the poisoning of the dog a foreshadowing of violence to myself?

Sitting there in the hushed kitchen, with

139

the clock loudly ticking away the minutes, I felt an icy dread spreading through my body. What next? I asked myself.

I didn't have to stay, of course. I could pick up the telephone and call Mrs. Canfield, give her one of a half-dozen reasonable excuses, demand what pay was coming to me, pack my suitcases, and go. I could get a job in Darwin, Portsmouth, Durham, anywhere. Waiting on tables, selling combs at the dime store, clerking at a drugstore — there were all sorts of jobs that held no threat or challenge.

Yes, I thought bitterly, I could run. Again. For hadn't that been the pattern of my life? As far back as I could remember, I had been running from some unpleasantness. Once, as a girl, I had come home midway through summer camp because of a squabble with my bunkmate over a pair of tennis shoes. And my flight from Vermont. I hadn't gone off to "seek my fortune," to better myself in the big city. Not really. I had run because all my friends were married, and, embarrassingly, I was not. One day I had overheard Celeste, a girl I had grown up with, pityingly refer to me as an old maid. The next day I had made plans for my departure.

And my "adventure" in New York. That

was a panic flight if there ever was one. I had turned tail and run, escaped from the city, from Dennis, from the fear of facing a competitive world.

And now I was ready to run again. Someone was counting on my timidity, waiting for my retreat. Anger replaced fear. No, I told myself, I wasn't going *this* time. Whoever it was, whatever it was, I was going to stay and see it through.

Then, as if in punctuation to my decision, the telephone rang.

TEN

It was Mrs. Canfield.

"Are things running smoothly, Miss Ferris?" she began without preliminary.

"Yes . . . yes, they are." I found I could not tell her about Orpheus. Not yet. I was afraid that her curt indifference to anything that affected me would only deepen my painful perplexity.

"Good. I called to tell you that Miles and I will be bringing a guest this weekend. A Miss Thornbury. Please prepare one of the extra bedrooms. She prefers the one that has the Jacquard coverlet." Apparently Miss Thornbury had been a guest before. "See that she has plenty of clean towels. A vase of fresh flowers would go nicely."

Where was I to get fresh flowers in November? "But, Mrs. Canfield," I explained, "the flowers are gone at this time of year."

"Oh, so they are. Well, find a sprig of berries. Use your ingenuity, girl. Oh, yes. We'll have supper at the house. The three of us. Get Dolly to come in and cook." Not can she or will she, but "get Dolly." "She'll do it," Mrs. Canfield went on, as if reading my thoughts. "Dolly loves to cook. Have her do one of her roast chicken dinners. Mind you it's not a tough bird." I often marveled at how Mrs. Canfield could descend from patrician lady to thrifty hausfrau without losing a smidgen of dignity. "I'll bring the wine and the fixings for martinis before supper."

"What time can I expect you?" I asked.

"We'll be there when we get there," she replied and hung up.

I called Dolly and told her of Mrs. Canfield's plans.

"Miss Thornbury's coming?" she asked.

"Yes," I said.

"Oh-oh." She chuckled. "So Mrs. Canfield is still at it."

"At what?" I asked.

"Why, she's been trying to marry Miles off to that Miss Thornbury since he was knee-high to a grasshopper."

"Miss Thornbury? What is she like?" I asked, knowing that my curiosity about Miles was pushing me into gossip and not caring.

"She's high society," said Dolly. "High society from Boston and with money. She's . . ." Dolly was interrupted by an angry murmuring in the background. "Yes, dear," I heard her say. Then to me she said, "Have to help Mr. T. now, Miss Emmy. But I'll be down early in the morning. If you give me a list of the things you need I'll bring them with me so that you won't have to make a trip into town."

On Saturday, for the first time, the sun did not shine. There was a leaden grayness to the sky, and the air smelled of threatened rain. The wind, when I went out to tell Damon to bring in wood for the fireplaces, was cold and piercing. It was a dull, depressing morning, brightened only by the sight of Dolly put-putting into the yard in her ancient Ford, her orange hair a vivid nimbus. She came bustling into the kitchen, her arms laden with sacks of groceries.

This morning she accepted coffee before starting her work. Over our steaming cups we again discussed the death of Orpheus. "Why should anyone want to hurt Orpheus?" Dolly kept repeating.

"Dolly," I said thoughtfully, "if there *is* a prowler or a tramp or whatever you want to call him wanting to get into the house, don't you think I ought to call the police?"

"Heavens, no!" exclaimed Dolly. "Mrs. Canfield would have your head if she knew you had the faintest notion of talking to the police."

"But why?"

"Because she had enough of police and scandal ten years ago when Arabella ran off. She said then that she'd never have another policeman inside this door, even if she was about to be murdered in her bed."

"Mrs. Canfield called the police when Arabella ran off?" I asked.

"That she did," Dolly replied.

"I can't see why," I said.

"Don't you remember my telling you that when Arabella went, she took everything but the family silver?"

"Yes . . . I do remember."

"You can't imagine what she went off with. All the jewels Mr. Miles gave her. There was a beautiful string of matched pearls, too. Some say it was worth ten thousand. And there was a diamond bracelet that could have kept you and me in style for years if we were to sell it. They had joint bank accounts, and I heard Arabella made off with *those.* She just about wiped Mr. Miles out."

"I can see why Mrs. Canfield would want the police," I said.

"Yes, she did at first. But then Mr. Miles got awfully mad. I remember I was setting the table for supper the evening after Arabella ran off. You know the dining room is right across the hall from the sitting room. Well, they were in there, Mrs. Canfield and Mr. Miles, having it out. The police had been there all day and Mrs. Canfield was fit to be tied because her pretty plank floor was all muddied up. And I heard Mr. Miles say, 'Well, if you're so unhappy, why don't you call the bloodhounds off? I didn't want them in the first place. I'm sick of the whole thing.'

"And Mrs. Canfield answered, 'Call them off and let that trollop get away with what is rightfully yours?'

" 'Oh, for God's sake, Mother. It isn't worth it, I tell you. I don't really give a . . .' I've never heard Mr. Miles so angry.

" 'It's Canfield money,' — his mother shot right back — 'and Canfield property, and I mean for you to have it back.'

"And they went on and on like that. I was sure Mrs. Canfield would have her way. So you could have knocked me over with a feather when Mrs. Canfield, the very next morning, calls up the police and says she wishes to withdraw the charges."

"She did? What made her change her mind?" I asked.

"She said that it was causing too much

scandal and too much distress to her son. Wasn't like Mrs. Canfield to let a little thing like 'distress' stand in her way when it came to money matters. But, then, Mr. Miles is the apple of her eye, and maybe she felt she ought to yield."

"But why did she get so upset with the police? Certainly it was more than just their muddy feet."

"*That* was a personal matter. You see, she and Sheriff Harris — he's retired now — never did get along. They once had a fight over a piece of property. Even got to court. Mrs. Canfield won the suit. Since that time there wasn't much good feeling between them. So, when this business about Arabella came out, and Mrs. Canfield changed her mind about it, Sheriff Harris got real nasty. Of course, he had to call the investigation off. But he gave out to the papers that he thought the real reason for letting Arabella go was that Mrs. Canfield didn't like her daughter-in-law and bribed her to go."

"Was it?"

" 'Course not. Mrs. Canfield just ain't that kind. She was fit to be tied when she heard what Sheriff Harris did. Threatened to sue for libel. Nothing ever came of it. Miles got a job that sent him to England for two years, just the week after it all happened. And he took his mother with him."

"Did they ever hear from her — Arabella, I mean?" I asked.

"Yes. Just once. Postmistress Haney told me that about a month after Miss Arabella ran off, there was a postcard from her. Some place in South America. Being a postcard, Mrs. Haney couldn't help but see what it said." (Remembering Mrs. Haney's bright, gossipy eyes, I could see where postcards would be irresistibly tempting.) "It just said, 'Having wonderful time. Love, Arabella.'"

"What did the postmistress do with it?"

"She forwarded it on to Mr. Miles." Dolly's round face was pensive. In the sitting room a clock struck nine.

"Nine o'clock!" cried Dolly. "Lordie, we'll never get ready in time!"

Although Dolly, technically, was only supposed to fix the dinner, she helped me wax and polish the dining room table, the chairs, and the sideboard. We buffed the floors until they shone. Dolly showed me where the good china was kept — real Canton ware, she told me. Although it looked like the more common variety of willowware, it was actually the forerunner of this popular design. Exported from

Canton in the late eighteenth century, this set of dinnerware had been in the family ever since. "It's got a long history," said Dolly. "But all I can say for it is that I would sooner break a finger than one of these cups."

It was pleasurable working with Dolly. Her sunny disposition and her spontaneous laughter put me in a party mood, even though I realized that it wasn't *my* party, not even one I had been invited to attend. "Am I expected to serve dinner?" I asked Dolly.

"Why, no, Miss Emmy," she said. "I always do that. Besides, I know just what and how Mrs. Canfield likes things."

I wondered whether or not I would be expected to eat in the dining room with the Canfields or in the kitchen with Dolly. Later, when Dolly set the table, there were places for three. It was a small, unintentional rebuff at my assumption that I was equal to breaking bread with the gentry.

While Dolly stuffed and trussed the chicken I went out to the woods to cut several branches of bittersweet. I was gone only a few minutes and never out of sight of the house. Yet, when I entered the underbrush, the silent, denuded trees seemed to close around me and isolate me in a scowling, gray-black world. I quickly found my bittersweet and nervously set my snippers to work. It was so unnaturally quiet. While I knelt on the dense carpet of leaves I found myself listening for the note of a bird or the crack of a twig. Nothing stirred. It was as if the brooding forest was concentrating silently on my every move. Was my unknown prowler, even now, staring at me from that clump of somber bushes or from behind the murky shadows of that tree?

The Canfields arrived at six. I did not know what I expected Miss Thornbury to be like — young and pretty, perhaps, with a debutante's pert smile, smart to the top of her latest hairdo. But when I saw her, I could not help but smile. She was the prototype of what could only be described as the "horsey set." Tall, gaunt, long of tooth, she appeared to be in her early thirties. Her blue-green tweed suit, I knew, had an expensive label; it was well cut, but it hung on her bony frame as if it were still on its hanger at the shop. Her face had a shiny pallor heightened by a spot of red on each cheek and one on the tip of her long nose.

Although she was only an inch or two

shorter than Miles, she clung to his arm in a kittenish way that would have been ludicrous had not Miles appeared to be perfectly at ease. In fact, he patted her hand so familiarly more than once that I began to wonder if Mrs. Canfield's machinations to have her son marry into society and money were not succeeding. What I would not admit to myself was that I was somewhat green-eyed at his attentiveness.

Miss Thornbury acknowledged her introduction to me with a cold handshake and then promptly forgot that I existed.

It was after they had their drinks and were about to sit down for dinner that Miles came into the kitchen. "Why aren't you eating with us?" he asked without preamble. "Dolly can dish things up. You needn't stay out here like a sulking Cinderella."

My face turned beet-red. "I didn't . . . know . . . ," I began.

"Didn't know what? For heaven's sake, Miss Ferris. This isn't the sixteenth century. Get yourself a plate and come into the dining room."

I didn't want to go. Miles' invitation had made me feel more gauche than ever. And I could not face Mrs. Canfield's acrimony. But Dolly put a plate and silver in my hands and literally pushed me through the swinging door.

To my relief Mrs. Canfield hardly noticed when I sat down at the table. She and Miss Thornbury were deep in a discussion on the relative antiquity of Wistarberg and Stiegal glass. Miles gave me such a broad wink that I wondered if he had had more than his share of martinis. Nevertheless, I was glad I had worn my green jersey instead of the cotton housedress I had debated upon.

But for all that, I might have been in the kitchen with Dolly. The conversation swirled about me, concerning people and places I did not know. Once or twice Mrs. Canfield would give me a glacial smile, a comment on the lovely centerpiece, a remark about the lack of rain — well-bred hostess duty patter. Now and then Miles would lean over and say irrelevantly, "And what do *you* think, Miss Ferris?" which only served to increase my discomfort. Miss Thornbury never noticed me at all.

After we had eaten, I excused myself as quickly as possible. I escaped to the kitchen, where I found Dolly at the sink, surrounded by stacks of unwashed dinnerware. I told Dolly that she could leave. I knew that she was anxious to get home, for it had been a long day for her. I did not mind cleaning up, I told her, since I had nothing else to do.

I was scouring the last pan when Miles came into the kitchen. I was keenly conscious of my flushed face, my sudsy arms, and my hair falling into my face as I bent over the sink.

"Thank you for the fine dinner, Miss Ferris," he said.

There was an undertone of amusement to his compliment. Had he enjoyed my embarrassment at the dinner table?

"Thank you for the thank you," I retorted shortly, "but I wasn't the cook."

"Oh, yes. The estimable Dolly. I'd forgotten," he said.

"But I'll tell her when I see her," I said, turning back to my pan, which I continued to polish with great vigor. He came across the room and stood beside me at the sink.

"Do that," he said. I could feel the pull of his gaze. Reluctantly I raised my eyes to his. He was looking at me with a steady seriousness. There was no mockery and no sarcasm there, only a compelling intentness. The minute between us stretched and stretched until I felt I was drowning and didn't care.

"Well!" he said abruptly. The flippant

tone returned. The spell was broken. "And how are you and your dog getting along?"

"The dog died," I said, turning my back on him. I placed the pan on a hook over the fireplace. "He died the first day he was here. He was poisoned."

"*Poisoned?* Are you sure?" he asked.

"I've seen a dog die of poison before," I said, walking back to the sink. "Yes, I'm sure that's what it was."

"Come now, Miss Ferris." Again the patronizing tone that never failed to inflame me! "Don't let your imagination start *that* again."

"It's *not* my imagination!" How could enchantment turn to indignation so quickly? Why did Miles have to be two different people?

"I suppose you think someone poisoned him," he said.

"I don't know." I wasn't going to tell him about my suspicions or about the watcher in the woods. I could not face his laughing ridicule of my "imaginary prowler."

"I'm sorry about the dog. Maybe," he said, patting my shoulder as if I were a child bereft of a broken toy, "you could get yourself another one."

I could have gladly thrown one of Mrs.

Canfield's plates of Canton ware at him. But he turned and left without another word.

Soon afterwards, using the kitchen staircase, I went up to bed. I sat and read for a while. What book I was holding, I never knew, for my eyes did not absorb a single word. Still seething over the encounter in the kitchen, I berated myself for foolishly yielding, even for an instant, to Miles' charm.

About eleven o'clock I heard the front door slam and the sound of Miles' car as he drove away. Mrs. Canfield and Miss Thornbury came up shortly, and I heard them say good night to each other in the hallway. I put my book away, undressed, and was about to get into bed when I heard Miss Thornbury calling softly outside my door. "Miss Ferris! Miss Ferris! Please come."

I threw on a robe and opened the door. She was standing outside, her tweed suit replaced by a long, olive-colored robe. Straight and narrow, it accentuated her tall, lean figure.

"Would you come into my room for a moment?" she asked in slow, deliberate accents.

Perplexed, I followed her into the bedroom. Once inside, she seemed to stagger as she made her way to the canopied bed. She slumped down on it. I noticed then that she was holding an empty coffee cup.

"I . . . can't" — she swallowed — ". . . I can't sleep." Her sallow complexion was strangely flushed; her eyes glittered. I thought she might be ill. Alarmed, I came closer.

There was the unmistakable smell of alcohol about her.

"Miss Ferish . . . I mean, Miss Ferris," she said, "do you think . . . and I want you to think *hard* . . . do you think you might have a drop . . . just a wee drop" — she held up her thumb and forefinger — "of cooking sherry? I need . . ."

The impeccable Miss Thornbury of *the* Boston Thornburys was drunk! It seemed impossible, but it was true.

"That's . . . all I need." She went on nodding her head to the empty cup. "Just one weeee . . . drop." She swayed forward and would have fallen to the floor, but I bent quickly and held her up.

"I'll get you something," I said. Was straight-laced Mrs. Canfield aware that her protégée drank? Maybe money and social position covered a multitude of sins, even for Mrs. Canfield. "Just lie here quietly," I said, pulling her legs onto the bed. She did not resist but sank down upon the pillows, the cup rolling from her limp fingers. She let me take off her slippers, and I was just tucking an afghan under her chin when she suddenly opened her eyes and grasped my wrist with a bony hand. "Think I'm stoned, don't you?" she said with a sly wink.

"I . . . just a little," I said. "You get yourself a good night's sleep and you'll feel better in the morning."

"That's shweet of you to care, Mish Ferish," she said while maudlin tears came to her eyes. "*You* care, but *he* doesn't. He doesn't give one — for me!" She used a word that would have disarrayed Mrs. Canfield's slick coiffure.

"Oh, Miss Thornbury," I said, "I'm sure he does."

How could I have been even slightly envious of this woman? Despite her drunken state, I could see that she was miserably unhappy.

"Ha!" She exploded with scorn. "He feels sorry for me . . . sorry . . . but *care?*" Her voice had become bitter, and the hard glitter returned to her eyes. "He's still in love with that horrible woman. Oh, how I hate her! Arabella! Arabella! If I could get my hands on her, I'd squeeze that smooth neck of hers until she was dead!"

ELEVEN

Miss Thornbury did not come downstairs until noon the next day. She strode into the kitchen, her bleached, angular face controlled and polite.

"I hate to trouble you, Miss Ferris," she said, "but may I have an aspirin?"

"Yes, of course," I answered. I found a bottle on a shelf above the counter. Her hand was steady as she shook three aspirin into her palm and accepted a glass of water from me. She did not allude to the preceding night's episode. I did not expect her to. It was hard to believe in the cold light of her composed, aloof facade that this woman was capable of such torrential abuse and passion.

"You've been very kind," was all she said as she handed the glass back to me.

Miles arrived at twelve-thirty. Mrs. Canfield had been fussing and fidgeting (she had called the Inn twice) for over an hour. She told me that she had reliable information concerning an old blanket chest for sale by an impoverished couple near Laconia. It was reputed to date from the early 1700's, and if this was true, it would be a rare find. She was anxious to get to it before some enterprising dealer made off with it.

"You're late!" she scolded Miles when he came up from the car to get her bags. "I told you I wanted to be off first thing this morning. You *know* . . ."

"Now, Mother," he interrupted calmly, "if it's the real thing, it's probably been there for two hundred years, and a couple of hours won't make any difference, anyway. Now you and Edith settle yourselves in the car. I won't be a minute. I want to speak to Miss Ferris."

Now what? I thought, as Miles closed the door on his mother and Miss Thornbury. For a fleeting instant there in the intimacy of the half-darkened hallway, his deep eyes serious and intent upon me, I had the turbulent sensation that he was going to kiss me. But the instant was gone when he said in a matter-of-fact tone, "Miss Ferris, I've been thinking over some of the things you've told me — the dog, the face at the window, the locked door. All those little . . . ah . . . incidents. Perhaps this place is too lonely for you. I wouldn't blame you if

159

you decided to seek employment else-where. Please feel free to go if you wish."

"Oh, but I don't want to," burst from me involuntarily. I looked up into his face, so near to mine, his fervent eyes, the angle of his cheekbone, his fine, sensitive mouth, and suddenly the workings of my own inner soul became crystal clear. It wasn't just my belated resolve to "see things through" that kept me at Canfield House. It was Miles.

"Are you sure?" he asked.

"Yes, I'm sure," I said.

He shrugged his shoulders. "Then, I have a suggestion to make. Why don't you take a week off? Mother won't mind. Go into New York. See some of your old friends. A play. Do some shopping."

"You don't understand. I don't . . . ," I began.

He waved his hand. "Money? Hasn't Mother given you anything yet?" He reached in his pocket and took out his wallet.

"No. It's not that . . ."

"Since money's no obstacle," he said, "I feel that you ought to take my suggestion seriously. Everybody needs diversion. A young woman can't be expected to bury herself in this antiquated museum. I know how these things are."

Did he? I wondered. Did he know what it was not to have friends, money, self-confidence? "Thank you," I answered. "But I have no desire to take a week off. After all, I've been here such a short time."

"You needn't be so conscientious. Go ahead," he urged. "Have a little fling." His eyes were mocking again.

"No," I said. "I don't think so."

"Stubborn, aren't you?" He put his hands in his pockets and lounged against the wall. "Take my advice. It would be for your own good to go."

Later these casual words were to take on an ominous significance. But on that November afternoon I took them for a thoughtful gesture — and was pleased because Miles had been so considerate.

Outside the car horn tooted raucously. Miles flung the door open. "Coming!" he shouted. To me he said, "Think it over." And he was gone.

The house now seemed emptier than ever. I busied myself remaking beds, straightening furniture, repolishing the silver, anything to banish Miles from my mind. But it was no use. Again and again I recalled the timbre of his voice and his eyes, one moment cruelly teasing, the next kind or solemn. How complex and unfathomable he was! I wondered what sort of man he had been before he met Arabella. Had he been gay and warmly uncomplicated? If so, it would partly explain why fun-loving Arabella had attracted and held him.

And Arabella? What was she really like? Clearly, the only person who had known Arabella and had borne her no ill-will was Dolly. But, then, Dolly, by her very nature, would never feel animosity toward a single living thing. Mrs. Canfield, I was sure, hated Arabella from the beginning. It was easy to see how a doting mother would resent any bride her only son had brought home unless, in this case (I remembered Miss Thornbury), she herself had picked the bride. But this bride was also an upstart, a woman outside Mrs. Canfield's pale, without a name, money, or social position. And I could well imagine Mrs. Canfield's quick, shrewd assessment of Arabella's greediness. How it must have rankled, too, to have Arabella look upon Canfield House with such disdain.

And the others, such as Damon (according to Dolly), disliked her heartily. Arabella had tried to have Damon dismissed, separated from his beloved Miles. There was no doubt in my mind that the mute, with his natural hostility to people

162

outside his world, nursed a sullen hatred for Arabella.

And what of the seemingly proper Miss Thornbury? I could not erase the picture of this gaunt-faced woman, disappointed in love for years, still bitter because *he* remembered only Arabella. Her venomous words, "If I could get my hands on her . . . ," spoke of passionate loathing.

Lastly, there was Miles, a proud, virile man betrayed, so guilelessly made the fool. No wonder contempt glared from his eyes and mockery twisted his smile. Even so, I sensed that his hate for her was tempered still by the thought of her seductive presence. If she were to come back and ask forgiveness, giving him her warm body and soft mouth, would he forget the past? Was it impossible for him to ever see another woman because Arabella's lovely image was always mirrored in his eyes? There was no use in telling myself that Arabella was a vain, selfish creature. Although she was gone, her beautiful, tormenting presence remained.

Strange, how speculation on a woman I had never met could so obsess me. I thought of the room upstairs, the golden poppies entwined upon the walls, the wide expanse of satiny bed, and how afraid I had been when I had walked through the door.

And yet, I knew that I was making my-self foolishly miserable over a phantom, a woman who only existed in the minds of others. Why should I brood over a past that wasn't even mine? Was I, sitting alone in this house, stimulated by Dolly's penchant for romancing, building a fantasy that had no foundation in reality? Suddenly my dark reverie seemed absurd. I could not, would not, go on in this non-sensical fashion, I told myself.

The impulse came to me to go up to Arabella's room. I would give it the cleaning it had so long needed. I would sweep away the dust and the cobwebs, if only to prove to myself that her memory meant nothing to me.

Armed with dust mop, vacuum, and furniture wax, I marched up the stairs. Undeterred by the sensation of chill (the room was merely unheated, I told myself) as I entered, I set briskly about my task. I set the vacuum humming across the carpet. The cobwebs were swept aside by a vigorous mop. I plumped up the pillows on the chaise lounge. Working quickly, almost frantically, I found myself fighting the same vague, unnameable terror that threatened to engulf me earlier. *I don't like this room.*

There is something very wrong here. An evil I can't explain, a small voice inside me cried while I hurried about with dust mop and vacuum.

I was on my hands and knees, trying to squeeze the vacuum under the dressing table, when I saw a train case pushed back against the far wall. I pulled it out. It was small and white, the kind used for cosmetics and jewelry. Automatically, I pressed the clasps. It popped open easily. There, nestling in white satin pockets, were creams, powders, lipsticks, eye makeup, all the paraphernalia used by a woman whose face is of great importance to her. There was no jewelry. I sat staring dumbly at the opened case. The large gold monogrammed "A" on the lid told me that it was Arabella's. And it had been packed for an extended trip. A trip that had been taken ten years ago!

Had Arabella run off and forgotten her case in the excitement of her illicit elopement? But from what I knew of her, it did not make sense. I had read of women stranded in the frozen Arctic, abandoning sinking ships, fleeing from burning hotels, who would not be parted from their cosmetic cases. I felt that Arabella Canfield, vain and proud of her beauty, would be one of these. Why, then, had she left it behind, shoved under her dressing table?

Something else caught my eye. In pulling the train case out from the wall, I had brought, rolling before it, two small pearls. Luminescent, identical, they rested in the palm of my hand. Hadn't Dolly spoken of a string of matched pearls Miles had given Arabella? The pearls, like two tiny sightless eyes, brought a tremor of instant distaste to my lips.

Suddenly all my firm resolution to dispel Arabella's memory vanished. The heavy, sweet air pressed a band of fear around my heart. I got to my feet with trembling legs. The hushed silence of the room, like the woods when I had gathered bittersweet the day before, seemed imbued with a malevolence. I was badly frightened, and I didn't know of what.

I thrust the two pearls into the pocket of my apron, gathered my cleaning equipment, shoved the case under the dressing table with my foot, and hurried from the room. The strange part of my fright was that once I had closed the door, panic left me.

Later in the kitchen, warmed by a cup of soup, I thought of Arabella's gold monogrammed case. Had she had it stolen somewhere en route? Perhaps the thief had removed the jewelry (assuming there had been jewelry in it) and had the case returned to Canfield House. I had to admit that my explanation was a bit farfetched. But I could not think of anything more plausible to replace it.

The pearls were more easily understood. Arabella had apparently broken her famous necklace and had failed to retrieve all the pearls. They were valuable gems if Dolly's estimate was true, but two missing would not greatly detract from the value of the whole. Could it be, however, that there were other jewels hidden in the room? No, Arabella would have taken everything. But suppose someone knew that she hadn't? If she had been in such a fever to leave, suppose she had overlooked a bracelet or a ring? There might be a hidden drawer or a secret cupboard where her valuables had been kept. Was that why I had caught someone unawares behind the locked door of Arabella's room? But who? Who would know about concealed hiding places? And, answering my own question, I enumerated: Mrs. Canfield, Miles, and Arabella's lover.

Then it came to me that I didn't even know whom Arabella had run away with. There was actually very little I did know about Arabella's hasty departure. Maybe it was none of my business, but by now I felt that I was sufficiently involved in the Can-field mystery to be enlightened. And no one could do it better, I thought, than Dolly. As the next day was Monday, I would ask her when she came.

No sooner did Dolly come panting through the door than I pounced on her. "Dolly," I said, "I found something yesterday in Arabella's room."

She raised her eyebrows. "You were in *there?*"

"Yes. And I found Arabella's cosmetic case. It was shoved under the dressing table," I said.

"But how . . . ?"

"Never mind how. I just did. And I found these, too." I showed her the pearls.

"Oooh," said Dolly, letting her breath out slowly. "From her necklace, those are. Well, that's strange, isn't it?"

"What do you make of it?" I asked.

"She could have broken her necklace, you know. She probably picked up all the pearls she could find. In that rug it wouldn't be easy, especially if she was in a hurry."

"Yes, yes. That's possible. But the case?" I said.

She pursed her small mouth, and a little

frown appeared on her smooth forehead. "I don't really know — but maybe she decided she had enough luggage. She *took* an awful lot. She had two mink coats and dozens of dresses, each with shoes to match. Maybe that extra case was just too much. I mean, she could always pick up another lipstick . . . ," she ended.

The answer, I knew, didn't satisfy either of us.

"You never told me," I said, "but who did Arabella Canfield run away with?"

"Didn't I?" she asked in surprise.

I shook my head.

"Well," she said, sighing with what I thought was relief. The mystery of the train case, a thing she couldn't explain, was too worrisome. Dolly disliked dealing with imponderables. Now she was on firmer ground. "He was a young, good-looking fellow, name of Steve Morley. He wasn't one of us. What I mean is, he didn't come from Tayburn or anywhere close."

"Where did he come from?" I asked.

"New York, far as I know. He was a friend of Miss Arabella's. Her tennis instructor."

"Tennis instructor?"

"Yes, he taught the ladies tennis at some kind of club the Canfields belonged to. He had the most beautiful brown curly hair — for a man, you know — and dark, snapping eyes."

"Are you sure Arabella ran away with *him?*" I asked.

"Why wouldn't I be sure? Didn't I find the note?" she asked incredulously.

"A note? She left a note?"

Dolly's chins quivered as she shook her head. "Yes, and I remember every word of it. It said . . ."

"Dolly," I interrupted, "it would all make more sense to me if you told me what happened from the very beginning."

"There isn't really a whole lot to tell," she said, settling down to the cup of coffee I poured for her. "I've already said how Mr. Miles met and married Miss Arabella. How she hated it here, even though they'd only come for weekends. Mrs. Canfield stayed here most of the time when she wasn't going off on jaunts with Miss Thornbury. Then one weekend Mr. Miles, Miss Arabella, and Steve Morley came up. Mrs. Canfield was here, too. I served their supper that night and right away I could feel the sparks flying between Miss Arabella and that Morley. They was joking back and forth. Oh, he was one could charm a dog off a meat wagon."

"Didn't Mr. Canfield . . . ?" I began.

"Didn't even seem to notice. I think his mother did. But, you see, Mr. Miles was that much in love. Didn't ever occur to him that Miss Arabella wouldn't feel the same. Besides, he was . . . well, kind of used to being his Mama's idol. And, I suppose, when he was married, he more or less thought he'd be the same with his wife."

"I . . . see."

"It wasn't long after," she went on, "that Mrs. Canfield went off to Canada. I think it was with Miss Thornbury. Miss Arabella took to coming up to the house during the week. She came alone. I thought it was kind of funny. But she stopped in the store and told me she could manage herself. 'Don't bother to come up, Dolly,' she said, 'except on weekends when Miles is with me.'

"And then one day I saw this low, long red car stopped for gas across the street at the feed store. And who would be driving it but this fellow Mr. Morley. He had one of them jaunty caps over his snapping eyes; but I recognized him."

"Did he come often?" I asked.

"I can't say for sure. Because, you see, there is another road into Canfield House.

It's rough, but it can be used. It goes through Darwin and comes out near Canfield through the woods."

I remembered the pitted rough road that ran through the brook.

"It wasn't two, maybe three weeks after Steve Morley came for dinner that the two of them ran off."

"Did you happen to see them go?"

"No. No one did. But I know *when* they went. It was late September — the last week, if I remember correctly. Miss Arabella came by on a Tuesday, stopping for cigarettes. Nothing else. No groceries or anything. I waited on her. Mr. T. was busy with the ledger. I can remember it all clearly now. She was wearing a red dress, her golden hair hanging down to her shoulders. She was all excited about something. Nervous, too. But I didn't notice it much on that day. It was only afterwards I remembered. 'Dolly, old girl,' I recall her saying, 'I think my horoscope's finally tuned in right. Today is my lucky day.' I was interested in astrology then, and so was Miss Arabella. We both happened to be born under the same sign, Aries. We neither of us took it serious but just kidded each other. So how was I to know what she was really trying to tell me? I hadn't the least notion in the world that that was the very last day I would ever see her."

"It puzzles me," I said to Dolly, "why the police never found the case or the pearls."

"The police?" she asked.

"Why, yes. Didn't you tell me the police were called in by Mrs. Canfield?"

"They were called in, all right. But Mr. Miles absolutely forbade them to search Arabella's room. He said that he had already made a thorough search, and it wasn't necessary for anyone to go tramping through there. He wouldn't even give them a list of jewelry she had taken. 'After all,' he said, and I guess he was right, 'they were hers, weren't they?' "

Dolly paused, staring into her empty coffee cup. "The day after Arabella came into the store," she went on, "I got a call from Mr. Miles. 'Dolly,' he said, 'I want you to go up to the house. I've been trying to get Arabella on the phone all morning. I know she's there. She might be sick, or maybe she's had an accident.'

" 'Sure, Mr. Canfield,' I said, 'I'll go right away.'

"Mr. T. was feeling under the weather that morning, as I recall, and he didn't like me leaving the store. 'Why do you have to run every time them Canfields snap their

173

fingers? If Mr. Canfield wants to know about his wife, let him go himself,' he said. But, of course, I *couldn't* do anything but what Mr. Miles wanted.

"As soon as I drove up I knew something was wrong. Miss Arabella's car was sitting there, all right, one of them white convertible jobs. Damon wasn't anywhere around, but, then, as you noticed, he keeps pretty much to himself, anyway. But the house was so quiet. All the blinds were down, although it was past eleven. She's probably sleeping late, I told myself, and didn't hear the telephone.

"I let myself in the kitchen. Not a pot, pan, or cup out of place. Least she hadn't eaten anything. 'Miss Arabella! Miss Arabella!' I remember hollering at the bottom of the steps. I never got over that feeling of something wrong. Even before I went up them steps, I just *knew*. I knocked on her door. No answer. I went in. And there everything was, neat and tidy as a pin, as if Miss Arabella hadn't been there for weeks. The bed made up smooth, just the way *I* do it, with the spread tucked roundlike over the pillows.

"And then I saw the note on her dressing table. It wasn't in an envelope or anything. Just a sheet of that gold-speckled paper

174

Arabella liked to use. I came to know that note by heart. I read it when I found it and then again when I called Mr. Miles. It said, 'Miles, darling. I hate to do this to you, but I simply couldn't stand married life another moment. Steve and I are going off. Europe, South America, the South Seas, some *fun* place. I'm taking a few things with me. Hope you don't mind, but really, my two years were worth *something*.' "

"How did Mr. Canfield take it? I mean, when you read the note," I said.

"He didn't get excited or lose his temper, if that's what you mean. He didn't say anything. Just 'Thank you, Dolly.' " She rose and carried our empty coffee cups to the sink. She rinsed the cups under the tap. Then she reached for a handkerchief in her apron pocket and blew her nose loudly. I went up to her, for I knew our talk had upset her.

"I'm sorry, Dolly, I . . . ," I began.

She put her hand on my arm. There were tears in her liquid brown eyes. "It's all right, Miss Emmy," she said. "But that's all in the past. Now that I tell the story, I know that it's best forgotten. She's gone . . . and the book is closed."

But was it? There was the train case and the two matched pearls.

TWELVE

Mrs. Canfield did not come to the house the following weekend. Miles called on Friday night and said that his mother and Miss Thornbury had gone to Bermuda for a "rest." "I'll have to come by, though," he added. "Mother has lined up some workmen from Darwin, and I'll have to show them what's to be done. She's bound to have those stupid fireplaces."

"When can I expect you, then?" I asked, trying to give my voice an aloofness I did not feel.

"Some time tomorrow, I suppose." There was a small pause. "Any more faces at the window, Miss Ferris?" I could visualize his taunting smile.

"No," I said coldly. (Couldn't he be civil for more than five minutes?) "Not since you were here."

"Touché!" He laughed. "I'm glad to see you have *some* humor in your prim and proper soul."

Before I could think of a stinging reply,

he hung up. For a long time I sat staring at the telephone. Why did he upset me so? For in my exasperation I had completely forgotten to tell him about the train case and the pearls.

Miles and the workmen arrived late Saturday afternoon. The workmen came in a ramshackle truck, Miles in his own car. He took them upstairs immediately. I could hear them tramping around overhead as I busied myself in the kitchen. "We'll skip the back bedroom — for now, anyway. So, you go ahead with the two middle rooms on Monday morning." Apparently, even now, Miles did not want Arabella's seraglio, his shrine to her, disturbed. I knew there would be a bloody battle once he and Mrs. Canfield came to grips again over that room. For I had overheard Mrs. Canfield tell Miss Thornbury that she wanted to rip out the carpeting and the wallpaper, and "restore" the room to what it had been originally. And for the first time, I thought grimly, *I'm on Mrs. Canfield's side.*

After the workmen drove off, Miles came into the kitchen. "I wonder if you wouldn't mind whipping up something to eat, Miss Ferris. I haven't had time for lunch, and

I'm starved. Scrambled eggs will do."

"Of course," I said in just the right faithful-employee manner. "It won't take but a few minutes. There's some ham here. I could make a nice omelet."

"Anything will be fine. While you're working I'll run out and have a talk with Damon," he said.

"It won't take long . . ."

"I'll only be a moment. I'll just eat here in the kitchen. If you don't mind."

I put the coffee on, got the eggs and the ham out of the refrigerator, an onion, and some green pepper. I worked calmly and efficiently. I wasn't going to allow myself any personal thoughts. I was the housekeeper here. Nothing else. I set the table: salt, pepper, butter, bread. Did he take his coffee black? Sugar, cream.

He came in just as I was lifting the omelet from the pan. "Mmmm, smells good," he said. "Aren't you going to eat?" he asked, seeing the place set for one.

"I'm not hungry," I replied.

"Come sit down and have coffee with me," he said.

I couldn't think of any plausible excuse to refuse him, so I poured myself a cup and sat down.

"You know," he said, buttering a piece of

bread with his strong, finely shaped hands, "I'm a little worried about Damon."

"Damon?" I asked.

"Yes, he seems to be drinking again," he said.

"Oh? I thought you knew. He always smells of whiskey to me, although I've never really seen him drunk."

"He never used to drink," said Miles. "That is, when he first came here years ago. But, then, in those days he had his friend — Schyler was his name. He was a little dried-up apple of a man. Lived in what we kids called the hermit shack."

"The hermit shack?"

"Yes, it's a one-room hut on the far side of the woods. It's still there, as a matter of fact. Who built it, I don't know. But Schyler used it. He and Damon got acquainted somehow. They would spend Saturday nights playing cards, drinking a little beer, just enjoying each other's company. Schyler didn't talk much, anyhow, so I guess he didn't mind Damon's muteness. Then one day Schyler fell and broke his hip. He lay on the floor of the shack for almost two days. When Damon found him, he was pretty far gone. He died that night. Somehow, Damon blamed himself. He was like a lost sheep. That's when he took to

179

drinking. Wine, it was. He got it from the Vestis, Italians who used to farm on the other side of Tayburn. They made their own. Damon would hole himself up in the loft and go for two or three days. Mother wanted me to fire him. But I couldn't. You don't turn out a faithful friend because he's miserable and sick." Miles shook his head.

This was the compassionate side of Miles that I had seen only fleetingly. It endeared him to me far more than his blond handsomeness. "I finally got him off the bottle," Miles went on. "I went over and talked to the Vestis — they've moved since — and then I put it to Damon. Poor fellow, I can't really blame him. He has to ease the pain of loneliness, living the life of a monk . . ." He looked at me, and the old sardonic smile returned. I suddenly busied myself stacking his empty plates and removing them to the counter.

"What beats me," he said, "is where he gets his whiskey. He never goes into town." He pulled out his pipe and lit it. "I'll just have to keep an eye on him from time to time." He puffed silently for a minute. "And what have *you* been doing, Miss Ferris?"

"I found something the other day," I answered.

"And what was that?" he said.

"It was a train case and two small pearls," I said, watching his features closely.

"And where did you make your find?" His expression was unchanged.

"In Arabella's . . . in the white and gold bedroom," I said.

His face paled, and two thin white lines appeared at the corners of his mouth.

"What were you doing there?" he asked.

"I didn't know it was forbidden."

"Forbidden? No. But that room is no concern of yours." He was annoyed. I had pierced his flippant shell, and somehow it gave me perverse pleasure.

"I thought it needed a cleaning. I found the case shoved under the dressing table. It was monogrammed with an 'A.' "

He did not ask to see the case or the pearls. Instead he stared thoughtfully at his pipe.

" 'A' for Arabella," he said. His mouth twisted into a wry smile. "Have I ever told you about my wife, Miss Ferris? She was quite a woman, quite a woman. Had to make a conquest a day, every day . . ." His voice trailed off. I went to the counter and removed the coffee pot and the omelet pan, and carried them to the sink. I was suddenly embarrassed by his confidence.

But the next moment he slammed his hand on the table. "That's enough of *that*," he said, almost gaily. "I must be off, Miss Ferris. And I thank you most kindly for the wonderful meal. You are an excellent cook, Miss . . ." He paused. "By the way, you do have a first name, don't you?"

"It's Emeline," I said.

"Emeline . . ." He turned it over in his mind. "The name fits; yes, I can say the name fits very well."

It was hard to tell by his smile whether this was a compliment or not.

"I'll be staying at the Inn tonight," he went on. "A storm's coming up, and I'm just too bushed to drive home. I won't be coming back to the house. The workmen should be here early Monday. They have their instructions. If there are any questions, you can call me at the office. Laswell Insurance." He handed me a card.

I walked him to the door. Outside, the wind had already thrashed the trees into a frenzy, and their last leaves whirled about the driveway. Angry purple-black clouds scuttled across the pallid moon. "It's going to be a wild night," said Miles. "Take care, Emeline." He ran down to his car and drove off.

I walked back into the bright kitchen. With a sigh I ran water into the sink and began to wash the dishes. The aroma of Miles' pipe still permeated the room. It was as if he were still there, his acerbic smile changing to a compassionate thoughtfulness, back to a laugh, then back to a bitter frown. Close to me but unattainable.

Miles' lack of interest in Arabella's cosmetic case and the two pearls mystified me. He had not been faintly curious as to why they had been left behind. Had he known about them all along and been reluctant to discuss them? It was plain he did not care to talk about Arabella. He had cut off sharply his only allusion to her. Maybe, I told myself, the subject was too distasteful. Or maybe he just didn't want to discuss it with me. A fascinating, complex man was Miles Canfield, but a man, I reminded myself sternly, who was not one bit romantically inclined toward Emeline Ferris.

When I finally went upstairs, I sat near the window of my darkened bedroom. I was far from sleep. The turbulence outside and the stripped skeleton branches moaning and tapping on the pane seemed to match the unrest inside me. Now and then the sky would split with zigzag pencils of light.

Thunder, distant, then growing closer, muttered and grumbled. The storm itself did not frighten me. I was accustomed to the violence of New England thunderstorms from childhood. But there was something in the sight of the wildly tossing forest and its changing grotesque shapes that made me shudder.

I must have been sitting there for over an hour when I decided to go down to the kitchen for a glass of milk and a sandwich, for I had not eaten supper. I was descending the front staircase when I noticed a peculiar smell. I paused in the hallway and sniffed. The odor was stronger here, but still I could not place it.

I was heading toward the kitchen when I was shocked into immobility by the sound of a slamming door. Was it in the kitchen or in the basement? Every nerve stretched to a taut, humming wire, I waited for another sound. But there was peal after peal of shattering thunder, and I could hear nothing else. I moved my frozen legs and with a shaking hand found the light switch. The kitchen, flooded in light, was just as I had left it. The back door was shut and locked.

The odor was stronger here. And now I could place it. It was something like gasoline, I was sure of it. But where? Thoroughly alarmed, I stepped into the pantry, thinking that some cleaning fluid might have been spilled. But there was no cleaning fluid there. Nor was there any in the utility closet. That left the sunroom. I wrenched open the door, and the fumes hit me full force.

But there was something else, too.

Transfixed in a nightmare, I watched as a small orange flame on the chintz-covered sofa grew and sprang into another flame and then another. The sunroom was on fire!

A crash of thunder brought me to life. I snatched a throw rug from the floor, precipitated myself across the room, and threw it upon the growing fire. I fled into the kitchen, plucking a pail from the utility closet on the way. I filled the pail with water and ran back to the sunroom. The rug was smoking, but it had not caught fire. I doused the smoldering rug with water, and while it hissed and sputtered I ran back for more water. Again and again I made the frantic journey between sunroom and kitchen, not caring about the sloshing water, my slippery footprints, or Mrs. Canfield's precious rug. Finally I was satisfied. The rug was a ruined, sodden mass, but the fire was out.

It was only as I stood wearily propped against the wall, my lungs laboring for breath, that the full impact of the fire hit me. This was no accidental conflagration. Gasoline had been spilled over the sofa, the fire deliberately set. I recalled the slamming door. Someone had been here in the sunroom as I sat upstairs watching the storm. Someone who had thought by my darkened room that I was asleep had crept into the sunroom, prepared the sofa, then lighted a match. That someone was either counting on me to awaken and run from the fired house or, in desperation, was willing to burn the house down and me along with it. But why? And who? What terrible secret was there at Canfield House that had to be eradicated so monstrously?

THIRTEEN

I did not know the answer. But what I did know now was that the face at the window, the footprints in the wet earth, the locked door, the watcher in the woods, and the poisoned dog were all part of some diabolical design. Miles might have scoffed before, but I was sure that this latest episode was something he could not possibly dismiss.

Miles! He was at the Inn. He could come and see the gutted, ruined sofa. *That* wasn't one of my hallucinations. I went into the kitchen and, with fingers still unsteady, dialed the Inn number.

"This is Miss Ferris at Canfield House," I said to an answering male voice. "I would like to speak to Mr. Canfield, please."

"Mr. Canfield?" he repeated.

"Yes, Mr. Miles Canfield. He should be there."

"I'm sorry, Miss Ferris, but I haven't seen Mr. Canfield since last weekend."

"But he's *supposed* to be there," I insisted.

"I'll have a look in the bar. Just a moment," said the voice.

I waited, my fingers drumming on the counter. Miles *had* to be there!

"Miss Ferris?"

"Yes?" I inquired anxiously.

"Mr. Canfield has not been here."

"But he said . . . ," I countered. Disappointment drained my last ounce of strength.

"If he does come in, Miss Ferris, I'll have him call you."

"Thank you," I whispered limply. Miles had gone back to New York, after all.

Now I was alone. Completely alone.

Overhead the storm renewed its relentless frenzy. Torrential rain drummed against the windows. Blue-white lightning forked through the kitchen windows. One terrible, ear-splitting explosion of thunder sent my hands to my face. I was afraid, horribly afraid. There was someone out there in that wild, unholy night who wanted me out of the house at any cost, even if it meant my death.

I leaned over the sink and peered out through the rain-streaked windows. Flash after flash of lightning lit up the whole back yard. I could see the oak, its branches convulsed in the high wind. The barn was blanched white under the glare. In one moment between light and darkness I saw Damon standing at the partially opened barn door. He seemed to be watching the storm. Or was it the house?

Seeing him there in the flickering light, with my nerves stretched to the breaking point, I felt all my old suspicions and fears of Damon returning. Could it be that in his simple, drink-befuddled mind he had equated me with another woman? Another woman who had come years ago and who had been a threat to him? Would he so resent me that he would set fire to the house? But it was Miles' house, too, and I could not believe that Damon would do such a thing. But how rational *was* Damon?

The abrupt ring of the telephone jolted my tightly strung nerves. I nearly dropped the phone in answering. It was Miles.

"What is it, Emeline?" he asked.

"Someone set fire to the sunroom!" I cried. It was all I could do to keep from bursting into tears.

"A fire?" he asked.

"Yes, yes, a fire. I've put it out. But this time it was not my imagination. The sofa was soaked with gasoline and set on fire."

There was a pause. "I'll come right away.

It will take a little doing, though. My tire blew. Then the car got stuck in the mud about two miles from the house. Had a devil of a time getting out. The road into the house is pretty bad. I'll have to park on the macadam and then walk the rest of the way. Be patient. Keep the doors locked. I'll be there."

After he hung up, I went upstairs to get out of my wet, grimy clothes, wash my face, and comb my hair. Now that I had spoken to Miles, some of the strain had left me. His calm, assured "I'll be there" had acted as a lifeline to my drowning despair. Help was coming, and I wouldn't be alone or afraid anymore. I knew that my illogical calm — after my appalling experience — was due to more than the knowledge of assistance on the way. It was Miles who would be here, Miles, who no longer looked upon me as "Miss Ferris" but as Emeline.

I brushed my hair and applied lipstick carefully. The navy wool skirt and a bright yellow sweater would do, I thought. Yellow was one of my most flattering colors; it brought out the darkness of my eyes and my hair. I studied myself in the mirror. I wasn't old or unattractive. *Why not,* I asked myself. *Why shouldn't Miles care for me?* Once or twice I had caught him viewing me with more than casual interest. Was it so impossible to think that he would look upon me as a woman rather than as his mother's housekeeper?

I was wrenched back to reality by the sudden memory of Father's stern but quiet voice saying, "Be sensible, Emmy. Stop wool-gathering." How often in the past had he said that? And wouldn't he be saying it now? Because a man like Miles had called me by my first name, I was weaving an illusion that had no basis in reality. I sighed and put my childishly romantic dream back into its rightful compartment.

Downstairs again, I started a pot of coffee. The awful thunder had ceased, but lightning still flickered, and the rain lashed against the windows. Miles would have a wet walk.

When he came, he was wearing a sou'-wester and an old black raincoat. Water coursed in tiny rivulets from the brim of his hat. "Borrowed these from Ben at the Inn," he explained as he shrugged out of the coat. On his legs were a pair of cracked hip boots. "These, too." He sat as he tugged them off. "Bet Ben hasn't fished in twenty years. They smell." He wrinkled his fine nose.

"Now. Where was your fire?" he asked.

I took him into the sunroom. I could not help the feeling of small triumph as I showed him the singed rug. The smell of gasoline was still strong.

Miles said nothing, his face impassive.

"Do you believe me now?" I asked.

"Yes, Emeline, I do. Strange, isn't it?" He poked about the sofa, then examined the floor. "How did you put it out?"

I told him.

"I suppose you mopped up the floor?" he asked.

"Well, yes, I did," I answered.

"And you didn't notice anything else? A gasoline can? Footprints?"

"Why, no, I could only think of the fire and I was scared it would spread to the rest of the house," I said.

"Yes, I can see that." He looked at me closely. "Did you happen to look outside at all?"

"No, not at first. I did hear a door slam before I got to the kitchen. But it wasn't the kitchen door. It was locked and bolted," I explained.

"Where do you think the sound of a slamming door came from?" There was a strange, guarded look in his eyes that I hadn't noticed before.

"I don't know . . . I . . . the cellar, perhaps. It wasn't upstairs . . . it was here . . . somewhere . . ." I tried to recall.

"You said you hadn't been to bed before you came down to the kitchen?"

I shook my head in the affirmative.

"So that you were wide awake and perfectly aware . . ."

"I wasn't dreaming," I interrupted hotly. Was he going to tell me again that I had imagined the whole thing? "I was perfectly aware of a slamming door. And certainly the fire was real enough."

"Yes," he said. "Real enough. Tell me, you said that you didn't look outside . . . at first. Did you look out later?"

"Yes, as a matter of fact I did," I said.

"Did you see anyone?"

"Only Damon. He was standing at the door of the barn," I said.

"Damon?" he asked.

"Yes. I thought it a little odd, but then Damon . . ."

"Surely you can't think Damon had anything to do with setting that fire?"

"I don't know *what* to think," I flung at him in exasperation. What was Miles driving at? Had he, by any stretch of imagination, thought that *I* had set the fire? No, that couldn't be true. "Why is everyone so protective of 'poor Damon'?" I asked.

"Because the fellow may be simple, but he hasn't a cruel or mean streak in him," Miles said.

"Maybe not for *you*," I retorted.

He was about to say something in reply but changed his mind.

"I don't mean to accuse Damon," I said apologetically. "But the whole thing is so confusing."

"Let's have a cup of coffee, then, and try to get at this rationally." He steered me into the kitchen.

I got two cups and saucers down from the cupboard. "Don't you think we ought to call the police?" I asked.

"The police? Whatever for?" He seemed startled by the idea.

"*What for?* Why, someone tried to burn your house down. Isn't that reason enough?"

"Get the police out here in the pouring rain, with the road impassable? Because of a little blaze?"

"A little blaze!" I was at the stove lifting the coffee pot. I slammed it down. "A little blaze that could have destroyed everything here. All the lovely things your mother has collected, the house . . ."

"The house could burn down tomorrow,

tonight, anytime, and I wouldn't give a damn!" His anger matched mine now. We stood glaring at each other across the kitchen. What was wrong with Miles tonight? I had never seen him give way to such wrath. Finally his lips twisted into a painful smile. "All right, Emeline, girl," he said. "We'll inform the law. But let's wait until the weather clears. Tomorrow will be soon enough."

"You'll call the police, then?" I asked.

"Yes," he said. But his voice was without conviction.

I knew that he didn't want the police at Canfield House now, any more than he had wanted them ten years ago. And there was a reason for it, a reason that went beyond his desire for privacy. I was convinced of that.

Suddenly the man sitting opposite me was a stranger. He was a Miles Canfield I did not know. Not the arrogant, flippant, sometimes thoughtful, sometimes kind Miles, but a brooding, tense, explosive Miles.

I poured the coffee in silence. He helped himself to sugar and stirred his coffee thoughtfully. Finally he said, "Emeline, I want you to spend the night at the Inn. I'll stay here in case of more trouble, but I think it's best you go."

"But the roads. I may not be able to get out!" I protested. If the road was impassable for the police, why wouldn't it be the same for me?

"I'll lend you Ben's boots," he said. "I'll even walk you to the car. It isn't too much of a walk. Come, now, get your things, and we'll be off."

"I assure you, Mr. Canfield" — I knew that I sounded prudish, but I could not help myself — "I'm not worried about the look of things if we both stay."

He gave a short laugh. "My dear girl, such thoughts were farthest from my mind. I just think it best that I be here alone in case our arsonist returns." He got to his feet. "And I think the sooner you go, the better." There was an urgency in his voice that his bland smile could not hide. It gave me a queer, uneasy feeling.

There was nothing to do but go upstairs and pack a small bag. My raincoat, a scarf over my hair, and I was ready.

Miles was waiting near the front hall. He insisted on my wearing the awkward hip boots. He tried to press the sou'wester on me, but it was too ridiculously large, and I refused it. He took my arm, snapped off the light, and hurried me out of the door.

We were halfway up the drive when the

sky literally opened. The rain was a pouring Niagara; thunder and lightning crashed and hurtled across the sky. Without a word we turned and ran back to the house.

Miles shut the door on the storm. "We'll have to wait," he said. He reached for the light switch. There was a dull click, the lights did not go on. "Have we candles?" asked Miles, a disembodied voice in the darkness. "It looks like the power has gone."

There was a candelabra on the sideboard, I remembered. I groped my way into the dining room, Miles close behind me. He found a match and put a flame to the wicks. By its uncertain light we found our way to the kitchen. Miles poked about in a drawer under the sink counter and came up with two flashlights. "That ought to do it," said Miles. "We might as well sit and wait," he added.

We both sat down at the kitchen table again. I removed the uncomfortable boots, my coat, and my scarf. There was a constrained silence between us. Finally Miles said, "Candlelight becomes you. Despite your harrowing experiences . . . you look . . . ah, what is the old-fashioned term? . . . fetching . . . you . . ."

At another time, another place, I would have been enraptured, foolishly ecstatic over these words. But now something in Miles' manner, an undercurrent of nerves keyed to a tense pitch made his speech ring false. I doubt whether he realized what he was saying.

"You are most fetching . . . yes . . . in yellow. You ought to wear that color more often . . . I . . ." He stopped abruptly. He turned his head toward the swinging door and then back to me.

"I don't know how long this rain is going to last," he said, as if his train of thought had suddenly changed. "Maybe all night." He got up and began to pace from oven to sink to door, then back again.

"What are you so nervous about, Miles?" I asked. So intensely had his agitation communicated itself to me that I was hardly aware I had called him "Miles."

"Listen," he said, bending over my chair. "Can I count on you to do as I ask?"

The question startled me, but I answered, "Yes, of course."

"Then, I want you to stay here in the kitchen while I go upstairs," he said.

"But what . . . ?"

"I haven't really looked through the house," he said. "There might be someone concealed in one of the other rooms."

I shuddered, thinking of myself preening before the mirror earlier, with unseen, hostile eyes watching from the shadows.

"But the slamming door I heard came from down here in the kitchen," I said.

"That may or may not mean something," he said. "But I am going upstairs. And I want you to promise me that you will stay here. Don't get impatient if I take some time. Remember, *you are to stay here.*"

I nodded dumbly. His peculiar behavior alarmed me.

He went over to the counter and took one of the flashlights. His shadow moved in a changing, misshapen silhouette on the wall. The thunder, coming closer again, threatened and muttered overhead. Suddenly I did not want to be alone. "Can't I come, too?" I asked.

"No! Stay here. And I mean it!" His voice was hard.

He went up the kitchen staircase. After a time I could hear his muffled footsteps in the room above. Arabella's room. I strained to listen above the growling thunder. There was a heavy thump, then another. My body a tightly coiled spring, I waited for the next sound. A rumble of thunder passed. And then I heard the sound of heavy, measured pounding. It stopped. Now it seemed that every nerve, every pore, strove to hear. The pounding started again, louder, heavier. It sounded like a hammer. But why a hammer? What was Miles doing with a hammer?

I sat there for what seemed a century, hardly daring to breathe. The hammer (if that's what it was) would pound a few minutes, stop, then start again. I was rigid to the snapping point.

Suddenly I could not bear the waiting any longer. I picked up a flashlight and started up the narrow, steep kitchen steps. I paused at Arabella's closed door. There was an uncanny silence on the other side. It seemed that the loudness of my heartbeats could be heard throughout the house. I knocked. "Miles?" I queried. No answer. "Miles," I called.

"Go away, Emeline!" Miles shouted. "I told you to stay in that kitchen. Now, go back!"

But I didn't go back. Why, I will never know. Maybe the thought of waiting in the wavering candlelight of the kitchen was more than I could endure. Or maybe it was an impelling desire to *know*, a wish to *do* something to release my bottled-up emotions, bewilderment, and fear. But I turned the knob and flung the door open. The room was pitch black.

"Emeline, for God's sake, go back!"

I swung the flashlight in the direction of Miles' voice. Its penciled beam traveled over and past a litter of stripped wallpaper and plaster. Suddenly a brilliant, silent flash of lightning bathed the whole room. What I saw I shall never forget.

Miles was standing by a dismantled section of wall. In his arms was a human skeleton. A red dress hung from its macabre frame. A bracelet sparkled from a bony limb that had once been an arm.

I must have screamed. I don't remember. I only know that I turned, stumbled, and half fell down the staircase. Behind me I could hear the pounding of Miles' feet. "Emeline! Emeline!"

I did not care about the storm, the rain, or the thunder. I fled into the wet, howling night away from a horror my mind could not grasp. In mindless terror I rushed down the gravel driveway pursued by a stranger, a man named Miles. I never saw the dark figure that blocked my path until he caught me suddenly by the arms. I screamed again and again.

It was Damon.

FOURTEEN

I must have fainted. How long I was out I do not know, but when I came to, I was lying on the horsehair sofa in the sitting room. For a moment I thought I was dreaming. The candelabra on the table beside me made eerie, shifting shadows on the wall. They moved, beckoned, retreated, fluid with fantastic patterns of light and dark. I turned my head. Two forms — one tall and slight, the other large and burly — stood with their backs to me.

I closed my eyes again. I didn't want to think. But memory returned with explosive force, and my heart shriveled in terror. I was there again under the brilliant, charged light with Miles and the skeleton in his arms. *She was wearing a red dress,* Dolly had said, . . . *her golden hair hanging down to her shoulders . . .*

I shivered with revulsion. That bony, grinning thing had once been Arabella. I knew that now. *It* had once been alive — Arabella in a red dress, enchanting and excited. Arabella had never run away to a "fun" place after all but had been murdered, her body stuffed into a boarded-up fireplace, resting there uneasily for ten years. No wonder *that* room had caused my very soul to recoil.

Bits and pieces of the jigsaw puzzle whirled in my brain. They revolved about the one fact I could not face. A fact that refused to be dispelled.

Miles had killed his wife. A proud, vain, passionate man, he had murdered Arabella rather than give her to another.

But why had he put her in the fireplace? Was that the reason for his hurried departure after her supposed "elopement"? And could that be why he was so opposed to the police? It could explain his aversion to the room itself, his stubborn refusal to have it touched, and his lack of curiosity about the cosmetic case and the pearls.

It could have been Miles (and was it only a short time ago he had looked at me across candlelight, urging me to hurry to the Inn?) who wanted me out of the house all this time. Did he think I was a threat to his terrible secret? And the face in the window, the poisoned dog, the fire in the sunroom? With Damon as his accomplice he could have been responsible for any or all of those things.

Later, in a more lucid hour, I was to ask myself these same questions again.

But, for now, my brain was in turmoil. And through this turmoil there ran a faint, electric thread of uneasiness, like a nervous, humming wire. I reached for it, grasped it, and was suddenly jolted into awareness. I was in danger.

For Miles had murdered, and I had found him out. He had not and would not let me get away. There was only Damon here, his loyal tool, and no one else. I could scream for help, but who would hear me? I could pray and beg for mercy, but would a man who had killed once hesitate a second time?

A blind instinct for survival forced my body to a sitting position. Instantly Miles was beside me, pushing me back onto the pillows. "And where do you think you're going?" he asked.

His face was hard to read in the uncertain light. "I . . . I . . . thought . . ." I struggled feebly under his strong, pinioning arms. I thought of the grisly thing upstairs, and the knowledge that this would be my fate, too, brought a hysterical sob to my lips. His hand lashed across my face.

"You're staying right here," said Miles.

I went limp then, and he released me. A strange, fatalistic paralysis washed over me, penetrating to the very marrow of my being. There was no hope of escape. How could I? With Damon and Miles watching, my every movement was under scrutiny. They would crush me like an insect, even if I dared to get as far as the door.

How had I ever thought I could love a man like Miles? How could I have been foolish enough to build such schoolgirl dreams around this masculine charmer? But I had done it before, with Dennis, I thought bitterly. It seemed an ironic destiny and now an ironic fate. The dreams had ended, and soon, too, the dreamer.

I watched through half-opened eyes as Miles beckoned to Damon. He whispered something to him, and Damon left the room. I could hear him mounting the stairs.

Was he going to bring Arabella down and bury her in the woods? For the fireplace was no longer safe. I remembered that the workmen were to come on Monday morning. Would Damon be digging a double grave? I turned my face to the wall and closed my eyes, no longer able to bear the sight of Miles, of the room, of anything.

Through a distorted dreamlike trance I heard Damon's footsteps returning and Miles' urgent whispering. And then Miles was bending over me. "Emeline," he said. I lay without moving. *Please make it quick,* I prayed.

"Emeline?" His cold hand reached out and turned my face toward him. "Emeline . . . I . . ."

He never finished what he was going to say. For there was a rustle at the doorway, and a loud voice shouted, "O.K., don't move. I have a gun!"

Miles jerked away from me. I was saved! I knew the full, sweet meaning of a last-minute reprieve. I turned expectantly toward the voice. The candles were guttering now, and all I could see was a figure dressed in a long, dark raincoat with a black hat pulled low over the face. A spark of light caught the gun barrel.

"All of you. Not one peep." It was a male voice. "Or I'll use this." The gun twitched.

"What do you want?" asked Miles.

"I'll take that bracelet," said the man. "Now!"

"Bracelet?" asked Miles calmly.

Suddenly lights flooded the room. Electric power had been restored, and I blinked in the unexpected glare.

And then Miles cried out, "Steve! Steve Morley!"

Even then I did not grasp the full import of that name. I continued to believe I was being rescued.

"So the criminal returns to take care of unfinished chores," Miles said bitterly.

"I didn't come five thousand miles for conversation, Miles. I want that bracelet," demanded Steve. He pushed his hat up off his forehead, revealing a dark, puffy, dissipated face that had once been handsome. His black, gleaming eyes were focused on Miles.

"What bracelet?" asked Miles again.

"The bracelet *she* was wearing." The gun made a slight motion upward.

She? I recalled the scintillating bauble on the skeleton upstairs. *She* was Arabella!

"There is no bracelet," said Miles.

"Don't give me that! She had it on when I put her in that fireplace. So cough up or you'll be joining your ever-loving wife."

Full realization knocked the numbness from my mind. This was Steve Morley, the Steve Morley who had been Arabella's lover! By his own confession it was he who had put Arabella into her unhallowed grave.

My first reaction was one of overpowering

shame. I had believed Miles a murderer. I had accused and found him guilty in a moment of unreasoned panic. And he must have known it when I ran from the white and gold room in such terror.

"So *you* killed her," said Miles. His face was haggard and drawn. "Why? Wouldn't she hand over the money and her jewels to you? Did she find out too soon that that was all you wanted in the first place?"

"I said to cut the conversation." Steve waved the gun menacingly. "Where is it?"

"Go see for yourself," said Miles.

"I did. It isn't upstairs, so I know you have it on you. Quit stalling. I mean business." He took a step forward. "I'll count to ten. One, two . . ."

Suddenly Damon, who had been standing mute and bewildered beside Miles, lumbered forward.

A shot rang out. Damon kept coming. There was another shot. And like a slow-motion nightmare, he slowly crumpled to the floor.

"Now you know I'm not fooling," said Steve. "You'll be next." He pointed the gun at Miles.

"It's in Damon's pocket," said Miles in a tone of great weariness. (So *that* was why Damon had gone upstairs.)

Quickly Steve knelt beside Damon. "Don't try anything," he said to Miles. With one hand he nervously began to search Damon's pockets, his eyes never leaving Miles' face.

I am not a brave woman. And what I did next was not an act of courage but a compulsive response. What inspired it? Anger, frustration, shame for my hasty judgment of Miles? Often, since that night, I have tried to analyze it and have not succeeded. But at that moment, in a burst of unreasoned passion, I picked up the now extinguished candelabra and hurled it at Morley with every ounce of strength. It caught him squarely in the face.

Then Miles was upon him. He wrenched the gun from Steve's hand and pinned him to the floor. Suddenly the self-assured cockiness left Steve like air from a deflated balloon. "Now, listen, Miles," he pleaded. "I'll just . . ."

But Miles did not hear him. He grabbed Steve's throat and began to pound his head again and again against the bare floor. I had never seen a man so possessed. His emotion-choked voice kept repeating, "You had to come back, did you. You had to come back . . ." Steve's face had turned a deathly yellow; his eyes were closed. And still Miles kept at it.

"Miles!" I screamed. "Miles! You'll kill him!"

He stopped then. He was panting, his fair hair hung over his eyes. Without looking at me he said, "Call the Sheriff, Emeline. And have him bring a doctor for Damon."

Somehow my nerveless legs carried me into the kitchen and to the phone. My fingers were shaking so much that I could not get the Sheriff's number, and I finally begged the operator to ring his office. The man on night duty answered. I'm afraid that I was not very coherent. But even if I were, how could I explain a skeleton found in a fireplace, a man shot, a murderer lying on the sitting room floor? I had to repeat my story twice before the man at the other end could reassure himself that my call was in earnest. "Sheriff ain't here right now. I'll have to rouse him. We'll get there as soon as we can."

"We need a doctor, too," I said. "I don't know if Damon is badly hurt . . . or dead."

"Lady, just hold on," he said, and hung up. As if there was anything else I could do, I thought numbly.

I went back into the sitting room. Miles was kneeling beside Damon, whose forehead was bloody. "Damon? Damon?" Miles called. There was a deep, guttural groan. "Are you hurt badly?"

Damon groaned again. His face was a ghastly green. He opened his eyes briefly, and his throat worked convulsively. Then he lapsed into unconsciousness again.

"At least he's alive," said Miles. "Get some hot water and clean towels, Emeline. I think we might stop the bleeding."

I did as he asked. I tried to concentrate on small irrelevancies — the shambles in the sitting room and Mrs. Canfield's anticipated horrified reaction. Would this large white mixing bowl do? Was the water hot enough? Should I bring iodine, too? If I kept my mind busy, not thinking beyond the present moment, I felt that I could survive this horrible night.

Miles had not moved Damon from where he had fallen. He took the towels and the hot water from me and bathed Damon's forehead tenderly. I stood by, stupidly helpless, watching.

Once Miles said, "That was good work, that candelabra." But that was all. If he had been angry at me, shouted, ranted, "Why did you run, you fool? Did you think *I* did it?" I would have felt better. His silence increased my guilt. It never occurred to me that he was too spent physically and emotionally for conversation.

After what seemed forever, the sheriff, a doctor, and several deputies arrived. I didn't know where they came from or how they had all been summoned from bed at such a late hour (for by now it was two in the morning). Sheriff Hunt, a big, handsome man with crew-cut, graying hair, wore a charming, affable smile, as if he were out on a vote-getting campaign rather than at the scene of a crime. But I was to learn in the days to come that the smile was a deceptive facade. For Hunt proved to be a shrewd, perceptive man.

"I'm Sheriff Hunt," he said to Miles, giving him a large handshake, as if they had just been introduced at a cocktail party.

"It's a long, rather involved story," said Miles, "but I think you will be wanting this man for murder." He indicated Steve Morley, who by now had regained consciousness and had pushed himself to a sitting position.

"I never laid a finger on her!" Steve shouted. His dark features wore a look of sullen defiance. "That dirty liar did it, and now he's trying to pin it on me."

Sheriff Hunt merely raised a bushy eyebrow, ignoring the outburst. "And you . . . ?" He smiled warmly at me.

"I'm . . . Miss Ferris, the housekeeper," I said. By now a great, intolerable weariness had descended upon me. I wanted nothing more than to curl up in some dark, snug corner, close my eyes, and shut out the world. To think beyond the fact that my name was Emeline Ferris required effort. But I was not to be let off that easily.

The rest of the night was a blur. Men came and went, tramping with unconcern (and wet muddy feet) on Mrs. Canfield's shining floors. Questions were put to me, gently but firmly, by Sheriff Hunt. I recall only vaguely what they were and how I answered. I suppose I told him everything about the evening from the fire right through to my telephone call. Now and then his sharp features would mist out of focus, and I would draw myself up sharply.

Finally, when it seemed I could no longer keep my leaden eyes propped open, he said that I could go. There was something said about an inquest and not leaving Canfield, but by then his voice was reaching me through rolls of cotton batting.

In some way I managed the stairs to my room. To my semicomatose mind it seemed vaguely odd to see the first rays of the morning filtering through the wet glistening branches at my window. I fell into bed and slept.

The sharp slam of a car door awakened me. My first startled thought was that I had overslept. It was broad daylight. The clock at my bedside table said twelve thirty. My arms and legs were stiffly sore, and there was a leaden aftertaste in my mouth. A hammering at the kitchen door brought me out of bed searching for my robe. The cold floor under my bare feet was like a dash of ice water.

Last night! Had it been real or just a bad dream? I looked out the window and saw the churned, muddied driveway. I recalled with vivid clarity the revolving lights of the sheriff's car — or was it the ambulance? And where was everybody? The house was deathly quiet. Had they taken Arabella away?

The insistent hammering on the door continued. I slipped my feet into a pair of slippers and hurried down the stairs.

It was Dolly. "Forgot my key in the excitement to get away." She was puffing. Her orange hair glowed under a black pillbox hat. "Otherwise I wouldn't have awakened you. My, ain't it terrible? I always *knew* there was something queer about that room. I was telling Mr. T. just this morning how awful it was that such a pretty thing like Arabella had to die that way. And you know what that foolish man did? He just put his hands over his face and cried. Cried, mind you! Him that never even shed a tear for his Mom. Goes to show you, men are the odd ones."

She took off her hat and jabbed the pearl hatpin through it. "Now, I want you to go on up and back into bed. I heard you was up all night. I guess there's plenty of mess to keep me busy. I know about the fire in the sunroom. I can start there. Everything is supposed to be hush-hush, but there ain't much you can keep from old Dolly."

"I'm so glad you came," I told Dolly. "I don't know yet that it all really happened. I feel so drained out."

"Of course you do, you poor dear," she said, putting her plump arm around me and gently urging me into a chair. "You sit right there. I'll fix you a little breakfast, and if you feel like talking, go ahead. Although, as I said, I know pretty much what went on. You see, Cousin Bill — he's in the sheriff's office — sort of let out some of it to his wife. And she came to the store first thing this morning." Dolly went to the refrigerator and brought out the bacon.

"Bacon and eggs do?" she asked.

"Yes, Dolly, thank you. I'm terribly thirsty," I said.

"There's some apple juice here. Now, don't get up, I'll bring it to you," she said.

She poured a glass of juice. "Oh, I should have realized, when you told me all those things, what was happening here, like the Halloween mask, and poor Orpheus dying so miserably, that something was *really* wrong. I guess my mind doesn't like to think on the bad side of things unless it hasn't any other way to go."

"It was Steve Morley all the time, wasn't it? He was the one trying to get me out of the house," I said.

"Yes, I guess it was. Although, mind you, I didn't get the whole story. Bill's wife could only tell me little bits Bill hinted at or she heard him say over the telephone."

"Where did Steve Morley manage to stay without being seen while all this was going on?" I asked.

"In the hermit's shack," said Dolly. "It's tucked way in among the trees, and nobody goes there. Not even the kids."

"I heard Miles speak of it once," I said.

Dolly's eyebrows went up at my inadvertent use of "Miles" instead of "Mr. Canfield," but she said nothing.

"Have you heard how Damon is?" I asked. "Is he badly hurt?"

"No, not too bad. Mrs. Washburn — she works up at the hospital — told me that Damon got what's known as a skull crease from that bullet. He's got a thick head, that Damon. It takes more than a couple of bullets to make any dent in *it*." She put several slices of bacon into a frying pan, waited until they began to sizzle and crackle, then stood poised with two eggs. "Sunnyside up?" she asked.

"Any way is fine with me," I said absently. Then I added, "Why do you suppose Steve Morley came back here after all these years?"

Dolly shrugged her ample shoulders. "Beats me. He said he came for the bracelet. Claims he never touched Arabella. He told the sheriff he found her dead when he got to the house."

"If Morley didn't do it, who did?"

"Mr. Morley could be lying. But he just don't *look* like a man who would kill a girl. Them kind of men, I mean the kind who would want a woman's money to live on or the kind who couldn't do anything for a living but give tennis lessons, they're usually too weak-kneed to skin a monkey." She brought a napkin, a fork, a knife, and a spoon and laid it before me.

"He looked threatening enough when I saw him. Waving that gun and shooting Damon," I said.

"Some is brave enough when they got a gun to back them up," Dolly explained.

"I guess you're right," I said. "Now that I think of it, all of Morley's courage evaporated the minute Miles took the gun from him."

"Besides," said Dolly, "Arabella wasn't shot. They said her neck was broken. Strangled, they think. Takes an awful lot of bad, poisonous hate to put your hands around a lovely girl's neck and choke the life out of it." Dolly's rotund bulk shuddered. She flipped the eggs onto a plate, added the bacon, and set them before me.

Suddenly I wasn't hungry. The food that had smelled so appetizing a moment ago now had no appeal for me.

Was Steve Morley capable of an angry, passionate crime? Was he telling the truth? Had he really found Arabella already dead? Then, who could have been motivated by such bitter hate as to kill her? In whom did she instill such a murderous frenzy?

"It could have been several people," I said to Dolly. "A woman like that would have many enemies."

"Oh, I suppose I could name a few my-self," said Dolly.

I stared down at the congealing eggs on my plate. I heard Miss Thornbury's impassioned voice, . . . *if I could get my hands on her.* . . . I saw Demon's implacable scowl. And, lastly, I saw Miles relentlessly beating Steve Morley's head against the floor.

"It's not possible," I said, half-aloud.

"What's that, Miss Emmy?"

"Nothing," I said. "Nothing at all."

FIFTEEN

The inquest was held at the county seat on the following Wednesday. I had never been to an inquest before and had never had any desire to be at one. The whole idea of a murder investigation was distasteful. The fact that I was to be a witness at this inquest heightened my nervous dread. My whole being longed to wipe out the memories of the last two weeks. But here I had to face those moments again and relive the terror of that dreadful stormy night; and I wished, when I saw the eager faces that came to gawk, that the proceedings would be short and as painless as possible.

But they were neither short nor painless.

An unused courtroom served as a backdrop to the slowly unfolding drama. Whenever I think of that day in court, it will always be associated with the black, twiggy branches that scraped against the high court window. For during the proceedings, which were, for the most part, monotonous and repetitious, my thoughts would veer from the subject at hand, and I would concentrate on the intricate patterns of black against a gray November sky.

It seemed that all of Tayburn was there. Mrs. Canfield and Miss Thornbury had flown back from their "rest" in Bermuda. Miss Thornbury, tall, angular, and graceless, despite her expensive woolen coat, sat stiffly upright next to Mrs. Canfield. She never acknowledged my presence or anyone else's; she sat there the whole time staring at a point above a picture of George Washington on the front wall. There was not a glimmer of expression on her equine features, and it wasn't until the last of the inquest that she as much as turned her head.

Mrs. Canfield, wearing a smart black beaver-trimmed coat with a little hat to match, sat calmly poised, every bit the aristocrat at a regal session. Only the frequent, insistent tic beneath her nose-tip veil marred her outward equanimity. When I came in and took my seat (the Canfield party had come straight to the inquest from New York, and I had come separately from the house), she bent her head slightly in my direction.

Miles sat beside his mother, his dark suit accenting his blond, unkempt hair. His pale, handsome profile would bend every now and then as he spoke to Mrs. Canfield. I willed him to turn and smile at me, but like his mother, he only nodded briefly in my direction, his eyes expressionless.

Dolly was there, too, her orange hair discreetly subdued by a purple cloche. She beamed encouragingly at me from time to time, and it was her round, jolly face I looked for when I later took the stand. Next to her, to my surprise, was Dolly's irascible Mr. T. His black, lank hair was combed neatly, and his flamboyant, gold-buttoned vest was covered by a dark gray pin-striped suit. His bulging eyes stared straight ahead, but he twirled his arthritic thumbs nervously. I wondered if he was worried about the store and how Dolly had persuaded him to come.

But, then, perhaps Mr. Tuckerman had come for the same reason that brought many of the others. Postmistress Haney, for instance, sitting in the first row peering over spectacles, her eyes darting from one face to another. (And *who* was minding the post office?) She was chewing gum vigorously, and I could guess that this, in deference to the "No Smoking" signs, was her substitution for her ever-present cigarette.

The coroner conducted the inquest. He

was a faded, wispy man with a balding head of thin white hair. His nondescript features were almost hidden by large, black-rimmed glasses. From time to time he would remove these and polish them absently with a large, not very clean handkerchief. His small, stoop-shouldered aspect looked more appropriate for a position behind a notions counter than the chair of first importance at a medical inquiry. But, though his voice was as toneless as his appearance, the audience listened with rapt attention.

Dr. Grove (for that was his name) established that the skeleton found in the walled-up fireplace was that of a woman about twenty-three years old who had died either by strangulation or by hanging. He then proceeded to explain (and here his medical terminology was lost on me) how certain bones of the windpipe were crushed in such a way as to prove how the woman had died. From the condition of the skeleton it was apparent that she had died some ten years ago.

Dr. Grove rustled through some papers and then began to read a report from dental records, which proved conclusively that the remains were indeed those of Arabella Canfield.

His voice droned on. The room was hot

and stuffy. I wondered that even Post-mistress Haney's diligent concentration did not slacken. But her jaw continued to work briskly, her bright, beady eyes darting to and fro. I began to speculate again on Arabella and to imagine what her last frantic thoughts had been as she struggled for breath. Did life seem especially sweet to her in that instant between living and dying? Did she think of Miles Canfield with regret?

I watched the elm branches moving outside in the wind, naked of foliage, and a great sadness overcame me.

Suddenly Dr. Grove's flow of words ceased. Steve Morley was called to testify. The people of Tayburn came to rigid attention. In the three days since I had seen him Morley's face had become even more yellowed and sagging. He managed to look alternately sullen and scared. He gave his name, age, and occupation. Dr. Grove informed him that this was merely an informal inquiry as to cause of death, and that he was not bound to say anything that might tend to incriminate him.

"I haven't got a lawyer, anyway," he said. "So what difference does it make?"

"I suppose you have been told that the court will appoint a defense for you if you cannot afford it," said Dr. Grove.

"Yeh. They told me. And what kind of a lawyer would work for nothing? Probably some jerk who couldn't get a paying client," said Steve. "All I know is that I didn't kill her. If I said it once, I said it a thousand times. I never laid a finger on her. She was dead when I got there." The corners of his mouth turned down in petulance.

"We are not here to decide *that*," said Dr. Grove, removing his glasses once again and polishing them languidly. "Just tell us how you found Mrs. Canfield."

"Why not?" asked Steve, shrugging his shoulders. "I might as well start from the beginning."

Steve told how he had met Arabella, how they had "hit it off" right from the start, and how they had planned to run away together. Arabella was to take all the money she could get her hands on, her joint savings, stocks and bonds, her jewelry. She and Steve were then to meet at Canfield House on the afternoon of October twelfth. Arabella had some clothes there and a few odd pieces of jewelry she wanted to take with her.

"You needn't go into detail, Mr. Morley," interposed Dr. Grove mildly. "It really isn't . . ."

But Steve was bent on public confession, and once the flow of words started, nothing could stop him. "I got to the house around five in the afternoon," he continued. "Arabella's car was in the driveway. We were going to leave mine — it wasn't paid for, anyway — and take hers."

Dr. Grove peered at him curiously. "Weren't you concerned that someone might see you and prevent you from going or, at best, spread an alarm?"

"You mean Damon?" asked Steve. "No, we fixed that up easy. Damon liked his whiskey or wine, whatever he could get his hands on. But Miles had put him on the wagon, and we knew that if he could get some liquor, he wouldn't be too nosy about where it came from. So Arabella smuggled two bottles of rye into Damon's room the day we were supposed to leave. We knew that would keep him for at least twenty-four hours.

"I left my car in the woods and went up to the house. I thought Arabella would be all packed and waiting when I got there. She wasn't in the car. But women are never on time, anyway. I didn't think too much about it, although I was a little irked.

"I went in the house and called up to her. But she didn't answer. So I went up the stairs. She was there . . . all right . . . on the floor, her eyes nearly popped out, and that gorgeous face . . ." Here Steve paused and wiped his forehead with a handkerchief. "Somebody had strangled her, and with bare hands, at that." He stopped and looked down at his feet.

"You found no garrote?" asked Dr. Grove.

"What . . . ?" Steve looked at the coroner quizzically.

"Did you find a cord, stocking, wire, or such that could have been used in strangling her?" Dr. Grove asked.

"No. But I didn't look. You see . . . ," Steve began.

"There was no question about her having committed suicide by hanging?"

Morley gave a short laugh. "Arabella? Not her."

"Did you notice the marks on her throat?" the doctor inquired.

"I didn't notice anything but that she was dead. I was in a panic, I tell you. Here I was . . . all alone . . . with a corpse. And nobody in the world would believe I didn't do it."

There was a swelling murmur in the courtroom. I heard Postmistress Haney exclaim in a penetrating, sibilant whisper,

"Don't believe him now, either."

"I didn't do it!" Steve shouted defiantly.

"Ladies and gentlemen, please," Dr. Grove admonished mildly. "Ladies and gentlemen . . ."

Gradually the noise subsided.

"Did you place Mrs. Canfield's body in the fireplace?" asked Dr. Grove.

"Yes. You see, I was afraid to run. Afraid to stay. I looked around trying to figure out what to do. I thought, maybe if I hid the . . . if I hid her, I could, at least, have time to get away. And then I remembered what old . . . I mean, what Mrs. Canfield said about every room having a sealed-up fireplace. In fact, Arabella had told me that someone had been in a week before to look at the fireplaces. There was a piece of wallpaper torn off the wall right there in the room. So, I tore some more of the wallpaper back and I saw that the fireplace was only boarded up. No brickwork, just a little plaster. I ran down to the kitchen and found a chisel and some paste. I got the hole big enough without too much trouble and put . . . her in the opening as soon as it was wide enough. I worked like mad, but it wasn't a quick job or an easy one.

"Then, when I got her in there, I cleaned up all the loose plaster and dumped it in the fireplace, too. I saw, then, that I would have to have some smooth stiffening as backing to get the wallpaper back on, so it would look like it was before. The old boards were pretty rotten and, believe me, it wasn't easy trying to find something that would fit."

Here Morley paused again. I could see the beads of sweat glistening on his forehead. It was as if he were reliving those frantic minutes, rushing from kitchen to bedroom, terrified that Damon might come out of his drunken stupor or that some unexpected visitor might drive up and discover him.

"I finally found some boards . . ."

"Just a minute," interrupted Dr. Grove. "This is a *medical* investigation, and these details are hardly necessary. You needn't . . ."

"I don't mind," said Steve. "Why should I? I've already told it to the Sheriff. I guess the rest of you might as well hear it, too. Like I said, I'm innocent. I've got nothing to hide."

"Yes, but, Mr. Morley . . . ," Dr. Grove held up a slight, thin hand, and then shrugged his shoulders. Morley had not finished his story. It was evident that he would not stop talking until he had. It was

229

easier for Dr. Grove to allow him to go on than to have him forcibly removed from the stand.

"Afterwards," continued Morley, "I took her purse, her suitcases, and the pearls. She must have been wearing the pearls when . . . well, when she was strangled, because they had broken and were all over the room. I had to get down on my hands and knees, but I got every one of them."

Every one but two, I thought, the two I found under the dressing table.

"I decided I'd go off just as we had planned. There was enough money . . ." He stopped here and glanced furtively at Miles. "I had my passport and I could leave the country. Before they would find her, I'd be long gone."

I wondered about the cosmetic case. Had this been an oversight?

As if in answer to my question, Steve said, "The only thing I left behind was her vanity case. I got what jewelry there was and just knocked it under the table. I had my hands full with the other luggage and a mink coat. The case was small. I should have come back for it, but I didn't. Now," he said, turning to Dr. Grove, "if I was a lawyer, I'd make a big point of that vanity case. Because it shows I didn't *plan* anything. If I had killed Arabella in cold blood, I'd've made sure of taking that case."

I couldn't see where his not taking the case proved anything but that Steve Morley had been panicky. If the room had been searched at the very beginning, both the pearls and the case would have been found, and suspicion might have led to Steve's discovery. But Miles had insisted on the police being called off. The room was never searched, and for ten years Steve Morley had been a free man.

"It hit me when I got into my car," Morley was saying, "that when I put Arabella in the fireplace, she was still wearing that bracelet. Forty thousand, she said it was worth . . . but I couldn't go back and do it all over again . . . unglue the wallpaper, pry up the boards. I couldn't. I knew that if I ran the risk, my luck would run out."

"Thank you, Mr. Morley," said Dr. Grove. "Now . . ."

"I went to Alaska first," Steve Morley continued, ignoring the coroner. "I figured nobody would ever look *there*. But I had a friend in Rio de Janeiro send a postcard I had faked. I made it look like Arabella's handwriting so that if anyone was looking, they'd really be foxed."

Steve Morley had stayed in Alaska for two years. He waited from day to day, expecting a tap on the shoulder from the law because they had found Arabella's body. He did not know that the house had been closed three days after his departure and that no one had returned. Finally he chanced writing an acquaintance in New York and felt him out on the subject of the Canfields. He learned that everyone believed he and Arabella had run off.

"When I found out the coast was clear, I took off for Rio. I lived there these last eight years."

"Tell me, Mr. Morley," said Dr. Grove, now leaning forward, "why is it you came back?"

"That was the dumbest thing I ever did, believe me. I should have left well enough alone."

"Yes, but *why* did you come back?"

"For the bracelet," said Steve, as if Dr. Grove should have known better.

"After ten years?" Dr. Grove removed his glasses. He regarded Morley with myopic eyes.

"Well, things were rough. I needed money," said Steve. "It's a long story . . ."

"I don't think that it will be necessary to . . . ," interrupted the doctor.

But Steve Morley went on with his tale. He had changed his name and settled down in Rio de Janeiro for a year of high living. It took just that long for the money (he did not touch the stocks and bonds for fear he'd be traced through their sale) and the assets from the various pieces of jewelry, including the pearls, to be spent. Then he began looking around for a rich widow or divorcee. He found a divorcee, a Mrs. Hollis, ten years his senior but (as Morley put it) "loaded." Morley managed to be a fairly faithful husband for the next three years. But he became involved with a Parisian dancer; his wife found out, and she promptly divorced him. His divorce settlement lasted two years. By that time late nights, a fast pace, and drinking had faded his good looks. And he was older. This time wealthy, lonely women, although they appreciated his company, eluded him when it came to marriage. Besides, his known reputation precluded any promise of marital fidelity. He was forced to look for work.

After trying a number of things, he finally got a job conducting American tourists around Rio de Janeiro, sometimes escorting rich old women to nightclubs to put an extra piece of cash in his pockets.

"One day," he said, "I had a car full of middle-aged 'girls' from New England. After the tour was over, I noticed that one of them had left a Portsmouth paper behind. I happened to look through it and I saw this item about Mrs. Canfield. It said that after ten years Mrs. Canfield was going to reopen Canfield House and have the fireplaces restored. *That* made me sit up. The newspaper article also said that Mrs. Canfield was not planning to live there right away but would stay in her New York apartment until the work was finished.

"Of course they'd find Arabella, but they'd find the bracelet, too. I figured, Why not scrape up the money, fly back, and try to get the bracelet? I was sick and tired of taking yakkety women around, and I wasn't getting any younger. I didn't make peanuts on that job, and if the bracelet was worth forty thousand, I might be able to stake myself to a fancy apartment, new clothes, a sports car.

"I could get in the house, unstick the wallpaper (that part would be easy), get the bracelet, bury Arabella in the woods, then hightail it back to Rio without anyone being the wiser.

"But it didn't turn out to be that easy. Damon, I took care of — I just left a couple bottles of whiskey where he'd find them. (So that's where Damon had gotten his liquor!) But I didn't count on the workmen starting so soon or anyone being in the house after dark."

That "anyone" had been me.

Morley then proceeded to tell how he had tried to frighten me away. It was his masked face I saw at the window, his foot-prints near the dripping water tap. He had taken the chance of slipping up to the room (when I had gone off that morning) "just to have a look" to see if the fireplace in that particular room had been disturbed yet. He had jammed the door shut when he heard me returning. When I had gone to get Damon, he had slipped down the back stairs and made his escape.

It was his pipe I had seen on that dark night as he kept a frustrated vigil on the house. The dog, of course, was a hin-drance, and on the morning I was painting in the meadow, he had called Orpheus and given him some poisoned meat.

"I was getting pretty desperate by that time," said Morley. "I felt I had come that far and I wasn't going to stop then. I de-cided a little fire might be a diversion to get that lady out of the house. I didn't mean to burn the house down.

"I got in through a cellar window, doused the sofa with gasoline, and lit a match to it. Then I heard the housekeeper coming down the stairs, so I ducked back into the cellar. Just made it, too."

So *that* had been the slamming door I had heard before coming into the kitchen.

"I could hear her running back and forth, and I figured she was putting the fire out. I waited and waited. I heard her make a phone call. And then she sat down in the kitchen! It was all I could do not to go in and say, 'Look, lady this is a stickup,' because I had the gun. But I didn't know who she called or who would be coming, and I still thought I could get away with it without being seen. I felt that if I didn't get what I had come for *that* night, I wasn't going to get it at all. I had been lucky so far, but for all I knew, my luck might be running out."

Steve Morley had seized his chance to slip up the back stairs when I had gone to the door to let Miles in. By then the thunder was so loud, he felt that any sounds he would make could not be heard. He had brought tools and a large electric torch, and he had set to work at once.

"I was really in a sweat. By that time all I could think of was those shiny diamonds

236

on the other side of the wall. And I got careless. I didn't shield the light, and it must have been noticeable on the outside. Because when I was barely started, I happened to look over through the window. Right then there was a flash of lightning, clear as daylight, and I saw Damon. He was looking up at my window. I guessed then that he wasn't as drunk as he ought to have been and he had seen my light. First thing, I thought, he'll be coming to the house to tell Miles, and the whole thing is for nothing. So I crept down the front stairs, out the back door, and around the house. I didn't know exactly what I was going to do. When I saw Damon coming across the yard, I got my gun out. I thought I'd shoot when he got close enough. But instead of going to the door, he went around the other side of the house. He was staggering a little, so I figured he was drunk enough. But I thought I'd better watch and see. I followed him. But he didn't seem to be doing anything. He just stood bareheaded in the rain — and it was beating down like cats and dogs — looking up at the front of the house.

"Just when I finally decided I didn't have to worry about Damon, the housekeeper came flying out of the house, and Miles right after her. They didn't see me, so I slipped around back and through the cellar again."

When he went upstairs, Morley saw that Arabella had been discovered, and the bracelet was gone. Throwing all caution to the winds, determined to get his prize, he had come into the sitting room with his gun. He hoped, even then, because of the dim candlelight, to get away without being recognized.

The rest, of course, I knew.

"And you claim you didn't kill young Mrs. Canfield?" asked Dr. Grove.

"No. Why should I? I didn't have a reason to. She was glad to go away with me. Arabella was young and beautiful, fun to be with. I've done lots of things I'm not proud of, but I could never *kill* a woman."

"You'll have your chance to prove your innocence in court," said Dr. Grove.

"Maybe," he said, "I can. Because I'm pretty sure who did it." He paused dramatically. "It was Miles Canfield."

SIXTEEN

The courtroom stirred uneasily. Postmistress Haney bent forward in her seat and craned her stringy neck to get a better view of Miles. Dr. Grove rustled nervously through the papers in front of him. There was a rash of coughing and a shuffle of feet. Dolly stared at Miles in frank disbelief. Even Mr. T. shifted his protruding eyes to where Miles sat, indifferent to Tayburn's curiosity.

For myself, I could not bear to look at Miles. I desperately wanted him to be innocent. He *was* innocent, I told myself. And yet there were tiny seeds of doubt. I was ashamed of my distrust. Try as I would, suspicion kept returning to gnaw at my mind. Suppose Steve Morley was speaking the truth? Had he really found Arabella dead? Like a donkey on a treadmill, my mind kept returning to the same questions. What was Miles' real reason for not permitting a search of the white and gold bedroom? Was his adamant behavior in resisting his mother's penchant for "restoration" not adoration for the lost Arabella but fear that her body would be discovered? No, I told myself, I can't believe that of Miles.

Was Miles capable of murder? No, my heart protested, no, not Miles. But this man who had such compelling attraction for me, this man who could be alternately sardonic or sympathetic, was capable of white-hot anger. I had seen proof of it myself. There was no doubt that he was a proud, passionate man. Would discovery of his wife's infidelity goad him to kill?

No, not Miles, I willed silently.

While my mind wrestled with itself, Dr. Grove was vainly trying to bring some semblance of quiet to the courtroom. Finally Sheriff Hunt got to his feet, held up a large hand and said loudly but not unpleasantly, "Now, now, you folks can do all your talking later. Let's get on with it."

Dr. Grove murmured a quiet "thank you" and then turned to Steve Morley. "You must not make accusations unless you have reason to believe . . ."

"Reason?" interrupted Steve. "Sure I have reason. I think Miles knew what was going on between me and Arabella." Steve seemed to brighten now that he believed that public opinion might not be entirely against him. "If he didn't, old lady Canfield did. She never liked Arabella, anyway. She was always looking at her as if she were dirt or something. I'm positive she put a bug in her son's ear. And Miles could have gotten to Canfield House on that day before I did. He was always making flying trips up this way on business. What was to prevent him from slipping over, finding Arabella ready to leave, and then . . ."

"Mr. Morley," said Dr. Grove with a little more emphasis in his voice than he had mustered so far, "may I remind you that suppositions and opinions are not of interest here. And they would certainly not be permissible in any court . . ."

"That may be so. But I don't know who else could have killed her. A woman wouldn't have the strength. Damon was too drunk. I think . . ."

"That's beyond our scope here," Dr. Grove interjected. "Mr. Morley, if you have nothing more to say" — and here Dr. Grove summoned every ounce of determination — "of a *factual* nature, you may be dismissed."

Steve's sallow face flushed. "If it's fact you want, all I can say again is, *I didn't do it.*"

I was the next witness. I had known be-

241

forehand that my testimony would be brief, my words an insignificant part of the whole. Yet, when my name was called and I rose to go forward, I was painfully aware of a ripple of heightened interest, the appraisal of dozens of pairs of eyes. I felt like a fresh Christian being thrown to the lions.

I sat facing the Canfields. Although Mrs. Canfield's haughty posture was still the same, her tic had not abated. Miss Thornbury, too, had not altered her position. Her pointed nose was still aimed at George Washington's likeness. But the two red spots on her cheeks had taken on a deeper, wider crimson.

I caught Miles' eyes upon me as I sat, nervous hands clasped tightly in my lap. They were sad eyes, deeply pained. My heart lurched once, and I quickly looked away.

Had he guessed that I was struggling with hydra-headed suspicions that refused to die? Was he blaming me for lack of complete trust in his innocence? Or was his look of haunting sadness there because his thoughts were still with Arabella?

I did not know. The confusion in my mind was becoming a torment. And now I was before the people of the town, people whose faces seemed a hostile blur, trying to hide the conflicting emotions inside.

I gave my name, occupation, and age in (try as I would to steady it) a quavering voice. For one terrible moment I did not know how I would manage to continue. But then Dolly's round, sweet face swam into view. The orange wisps of hair escaping from the impossible purple hat, the warm eyes, and the bracing smile steadied me.

I told my story, from the very first day I had come to Canfield House until the police arrived on that ugly night. I tried to keep my voice calm, my face impassive, so that not the slightest nuance would betray my inner turbulence.

Dr. Grove interrupted once and asked me to speak louder. It was when I was describing the first and only sight I had had of Arabella's remains. When I was through Dr. Grove asked, "Had you known the deceased?"

"No," I answered.

To my relief, he let me go.

I had just reseated myself among the spectators when the rear door of the courtroom was opened, and a man I recognized as one of the Sheriff's deputies came striding down the center aisle. He went up to Sheriff Hunt, spoke in a low monotone to him, and handed him an envelope, which the sheriff carelessly stuffed in his pocket. Seating himself beside the Sheriff, the deputy (whose rough, mashed nose suggested a boxing career at some time in the past) riveted his eyes on the floor, ignoring Dolly's frantic waving. I guessed him to be her cousin Bill, from whose wife Dolly had received so much information.

Miles was the next witness.

He began his account with the details of the stormy night he had discovered Arabella's body. He said that he had come to the house the second time in answer to my telephone call. The fire had disturbed him. He admitted that up till then he had thought my "episodes," as he termed them, were the result of an overworked imagination and my being alone in an isolated house. He interjected here that at one time he had even suggested I take a week off, hoping a change would calm my nerves.

But the attempt to burn the house put all those incidents in a different light. He felt, as I did, that there was a person or persons who wanted something at Canfield House. But even so, he said, he still tried to gloss over the fire so as not to alarm me.

As we sat at the kitchen table, the storm crashing about our ears, Miles' instincts told him that the unknown arsonist might still be on the premises. It was then that he urged me to go to the Inn.

Dr. Grove interrupted Miles and asked, "Mr. Canfield, if you suspected danger, why didn't you call the sheriff?"

"Because," answered Miles, "I thought if someone was in hiding, either in the house or on the grounds, waiting for a chance to do a more thorough job, the police cars arriving would scare him off. After escorting Miss Ferris to the car, I planned to come back and wait in the dark."

"Seems logical enough," said Dr. Grove, more to himself than to anyone in particular.

Miles then told how we had been forced back by a fresh outbreak of the storm. It was after we returned to the house and the lights went out that Miles thought he could detect sounds coming from Arabella's room above.

He climbed the stairs to the white and gold room. His light disclosed the stripped wallpaper and the unloosening of boards where he knew the sealed fireplace was located. There was no one in the room. He knew that whatever the unknown intruder was searching for was located in the sealed-up fireplace. He thought that it might be some old family treasure, real or unreal, that had attracted an illegal searcher. Why someone should risk coming in the middle of a rainswept night, with two people in the house, puzzled Miles. Nevertheless, even as he finished tearing away the remainder of the wallpaper and boards, he did not dream that instead of treasure or just debris he would find his wife.

Here Miles paused. There were deep lines etched on his forehead; his face looked white and fatigued. He had recited the events of that night in a cold, business-like voice.

"Mr. Canfield . . . ah . . . when you found the . . . ah, remains" — Dr. Grove fumbled with some papers in front of him — "did you immediately identify them as your wife?"

"I recognized her dress and the bracelet," said Miles shortly.

"They were Mrs. Canfield's?" asked Dr. Grove.

"Yes," said Miles.

"There was no doubt in your mind, then? You did not think that it could have been someone else?"

"I did not." Miles rose to go without waiting to be dismissed.

"Er . . . ah . . . thank you, Mr. Canfield,"

interposed Dr. Grove. "You will have an opportunity to answer Mr. Morley's accusation in court."

"I wouldn't stoop to acknowledge one statement from Mr. Morley, let alone answer it." There was an unnatural flush to Miles' pale features. "That yellow-faced coward would accuse his own mother to save his skin."

"Coward? Look who's talking!" Steve taunted loudly from where he sat flanked by two policemen. "Sure, with your dough you could get yourself a smart lawyer and beat the rap."

Miles clenched his fists and took a step forward. There was deadly fury in his eyes. For a moment I was sure he was going to leap at Morley. But Dr. Grove finally produced a gavel from somewhere, which he proceeded to pound vigorously.

"That's enough of that!" His small voice beat against the hubbub that Steve Morley's outburst had produced. "That's enough, I say!"

Miles, clearly fighting for control, turned to Dr. Grove. "Go ahead and ask whatever you want. I have nothing to hide," he said. He reseated himself and calmly crossed his legs, but the flush on his face remained, as did the hard glint in his eyes.

"I'm not the District Attorney," said Dr. Grove, almost apologetically. "I have no authority to carry on such a proceeding. First of all, you are entitled to legal counsel . . ."

"I don't *need* legal counsel," said Miles. "You are conducting an inquiry into the death of Mrs. Arabella Canfield. We've gone this far — I see that Jones of the *Tayburn Blade* is taking every word down — we might as well finish it up with my version."

"Well, then." Dr. Grove looked hesitantly at a sandy-haired man in the first row of spectators. The man nodded in the affirmative. (Later I learned that he was the District Attorney.) Dr. Grove cleared his throat. "Mr. Canfield, did you know that your wife was planning to elope with Steven Morley?"

"I did not," said Miles.

"Had you *any* inkling that your late wife and Mr. Morley were on ah . . . intimate terms?"

"I did not."

"Didn't anyone ever speak to you of this possibility?"

"My mother did. Once. But she never did like Arabella, and I just put her remarks down to that."

"Very well," said Dr. Grove with a shade

of greater confidence in his voice. "If we can go back ten years to October twelfth. Of course, we can't expect you to remember each detail. But can you . . ."

"I can remember each detail," said Miles cuttingly. Dr. Grove's gray-fringed, bespectacled head seemed to shrink within his dandruff-sprinkled collar. "I flew up to Darwin that day on business. I'm in insurance, and we had a big account to settle with a Mr. Thomas. I arrived at his office at about ten in the morning. We concluded our transaction at lunch. It was one in the afternoon. Afterwards I flew back to New York."

"I see," said Dr. Grove. "Then you must have reached your office around three, three-thirty, so that . . ."

"I didn't say that," said Miles.

There was a silent void for several seconds, and then Dr. Grove cleared his throat. "Ah . . . eh . . . but you just made the statement that . . ."

"I said I flew back to New York. But I didn't say when. As a matter of fact, I didn't get back to New York until eight in the evening."

Dr. Grove removed his spectacles, this time polishing them with shaking hands. "You must understand, Mr. Canfield, that

I am not the District Attorney, and you are under no duress to . . ."

"I know all *that*," said Miles. "But I told you I have nothing to hide. It just so happened that after I left Mr. Thomas, I bumped into an old friend, Bill Peters, at the airport. We hadn't seen each other in a long time. Bill was passing through, flying his own plane up to Maine for some deer hunting. We went out, had a couple of drinks, and talked over old times. The afternoon stretched into dinner. And that's why I was so late in getting back."

"Ah, then," said Dr. Grove with relief, "I have no doubt that Mr. . . . ah, Peters, I believe you said? . . . would gladly vouch for your afternoon."

"I'm afraid not," said Miles.

"But if he is an old friend, surely . . ."

"Bill is dead. He crashed his plane into Mt. Washington in a snowstorm four years ago."

Dr. Grove peered blandly at Miles. The courtroom was so hushed that I could hear the squeaking of elm branches as they brushed against the window. My own breathing seemed to stop. Had no one seen Miles on that fateful afternoon?

I wanted Miles to be, once and for all, proved blameless. I tried to tell myself that because he could not prove his where-abouts on the afternoon of October twelfth did not mean that he was guilty of murder. Steve Morley was lying, as Miles had said, to save his own skin. Miles was surely telling the truth. How many afternoons in my life had I spent anonymously, without someone to swear definitely that I had been at such and such a place at such and such a time?

Miles was dismissed, and another witness called. I don't remember who it was. Mrs. Canfield? Miss Thornbury? Dolly? I can recall only the dull, droning sound of voices, question and answer, the scraping of chairs, the coughing of a red-faced man next to me, and the sudden spatter of a November shower as it tapped against the window.

Finally Sheriff Hunt was called. Instead of seating himself in the witness chair, he went back to the table at which Dr. Grove presided. He leaned far over and whispered something in Dr. Grove's ear. Dr. Grove shook his head in the negative several times. Once I heard him say, "highly irregular . . ." Sheriff Hunt continued his whispered monologue, and finally Dr. Grove murmured, "Very well, go ahead."

Sheriff Hunt sat down and gave everyone the benefit of his radiant smile.

"This is not exactly in order here. But there have been so many things that were not, I believe, and in all fairness to those who were the targets of insinuations, if not accusations, and also to assist the D.A. in bringing an indictment" — here he nodded to the sandy-haired man, who had been busily taking notes all through the inquest — "we bring some of our latest findings out in the open."

There was another flurry of coughing and murmuring, and I thought I could hear the renewed cracking of Mrs. Haney's gum.

"Now," said Sheriff Hunt, "when the remains had been removed from Canfield House, I naturally searched the room. After ten years I didn't know that I could find anything. However, I had been told that the room had not been used subsequent to the deceased's death, so I thought I might be lucky and turn up something.

"At first, to my disappointment, I could find no letters. Either Mrs. Canfield did not receive any, or if she did, they had been removed or destroyed. But a more thorough examination of her dressing table revealed a note stuck between two drawers. I should like to read it for you. I found it very interesting."

Hunt removed a sheet of yellowed stationery from the envelope his deputy had given him a short time ago. It had been crumpled once, but was now smoothed out. "The note," said the sheriff, "is dated September tenth and it reads, 'Darling Arabella, I got the money, like I said I would. It's three thousand. All my savings. I'd be happy to *give* it to you. Not just a loan. Because I know how that old skinflint must keep you on short rations. She has all the money in the family. I want to see you soon. I miss you and I love you.' It's signed, 'Your own Dan.' "

Dan? Who . . . ? The only Dan I knew was Dan Tuckerman. And for the life of me I could not cast him in the role of ardent lover. It must have been one of Arabella's New York friends. Was it someone that Miles knew? And, even so, I could not see how this love letter — for that it was, despite its lack of flaming prose — had anything to do with Arabella's death.

"But that wasn't all we found," said Sheriff Hunt. "Naturally we sifted the debris found in the fireplace for further clues. In that heap of ashes, dust, and old bird

253

nests that had fallen in the chimney through the years, we discovered a button. Tests haven't been conducted yet that can pinpoint how old the button actually is. However, we can guess that the deceased, as in most cases of forcible strangulation, grasped at her assailant, and the button came away in her hand. It stayed there in her clenched fist until the flesh decomposed." Sheriff Hunt paused. He looked around and this time he did not smile. "It was a brass button with an anchor on it. Now . . ."

"Please! No more! Don't say no more!" It was Mr. Tuckerman. He was on his feet. His bulging eyes were stricken. "I can't stand it no longer . . . ten years . . . All right, I did it! The button's mine. Everybody knows about my vest. No use denying it. I'm glad you found it. Now it's all over! She was beautiful . . . and she said . . . she told me . . ." He stopped and covered his face with bony hands. "And then she was going to run away with that no good . . . She laughed at me. Laughed and said I was just a country rube . . . so I . . . her throat . . ."

His thin shoulders shook. And the sound of his sobbing broke Miss Thornbury's gaze away from the portrait of George Washington.

SEVENTEEN

Later Mr. Tuckerman made a full confession. It was a tragic story, indicative of emotional chasms that sometimes lie hidden beneath supposedly sober, restrained exteriors. In all probability Mr. Tuckerman would have lived out his humdrum daily existence tending store, stacking groceries, figuring in his ledger, and scolding Dolly if Arabella had not walked into his life. But she came into his store one day, swinging her long golden hair, to buy a package of cigarettes. She was lovely, provocative — and bored. Mr. Tuckerman was just another conquest to her, the object of an automatic need to reassure herself that men, all men, were in love with her. So she talked gaily to him — and smiled. She asked about his interesting vest, most probably, hardly listening to what he said in response.

Dan Tuckerman had yearned to go to sea. He had secret dreams of great adventure in exotic, foreign ports. Like his forebears, as Dolly had mentioned, he wanted to sail under night skies, over uncharted seas, to have the wind and salt spray in his face. But he was stuck behind a grocery counter, with plump, easygoing Dolly as wife, trudging down to Portsmouth once a month to watch ships with other men come home from strange and wonderful parts of the world. So to Mr. Tuckerman Arabella had been a miracle lighting up his drab, disappointed life.

He would find all sorts of excuses to see her, to talk to her. He took to driving Dolly out to work at the Canfields' in the hope that he might catch a glimpse of Arabella. Often he did. Sometimes Arabella would find him in the kitchen waiting for Dolly to finish up her duties. She would always have a warm word with him or a little joke that would set him to laughing the way he had never laughed before. He took her flirting seriously. He loved her; he was her slave. When she complained that she needed money for a sick sister, Dan Tuckerman swallowed the foolish tale whole. The letter Sheriff Hunt had read at the inquest showed how completely taken in the poor storekeeper had been. (This was the money he had later told Dolly he had lost in a "business venture.")

When Steve Morley first came to Canfield House, and Dolly had reported how "sparks flew" between him and Arabella, Mr. Tuckerman became blindly jealous. Fuel was added to the fire when he glimpsed Morley's red sports car flashing through Tayburn one bright September morning. He confronted Arabella with his suspicions. She had chided him for being so foolish as to think she'd prefer a "tennis player" to Dan's solid, manly worth.

But Mr. Tuckerman had not been entirely reassured. When Arabella came into the store the morning of October twelfth, so alive, so vivacious, saying that something wonderful was going to happen to her, his doubts were aroused.

He went out to Canfield House that afternoon. It was then that she told him he was just a country rube and "whatever made you think I could care for *you?*" She was running away with Steve, she said, and would he please leave. At first he pleaded with her, but she laughed in his face. Seized with an uncontrollable, demoniac anger, he shook her, and when she began to scream, he placed his hands around her neck and pressed harder and harder until she was silent.

He ran then. Back to the store, back to

fat, homey Dolly, expecting the sheriff's shadow on his doorsill. But the sheriff did not come. When he heard the story about Arabella's running away, his first reaction was amazed disbelief, then a compulsive desire to see where her body had been hidden. For he was sure that this was what Steve Morley had done when he had found her dead. But he controlled his compulsion and never returned to Canfield House. Instead he became more taciturn and more acid in outlook; and his hands, his guilty hands, began to show signs of arthritis. There wasn't a day, he told the sheriff, in all those ten years that he hadn't paid for his crime in fear, anxiety, and torment.

Afterward Dolly wept, copious, pathetic tears. And, as was her nature, she did not condemn her Mr. T. but pitied him. "Poor Mr. T.," she had sobbed to me. "He was really an innocent. He didn't know any better. And to live with such a terrible conscience all these years. To suffer so!"

I had not wanted to return to Canfield House. It was associated with too much horror. And now that I had seen the events that had so frightened me through to their tragic denouement, I could no longer accuse myself of running away. But, more than that, I was ashamed to face Miles. I did not know yet whether he suspected my headlong judgment of him, and I did not know how I would ever be able to apologize or even to explain my feelings.

As it turned out, my apprehension was unnecessary. Miles never mentioned the events of that dreadful night until long after it had receded into the limbo of bad memories. Mrs. Canfield had asked me to stay on, if only for a few weeks. "I don't blame you for wanting to go," she said. "But you would do me a great kindness if you could remain here at least until I can get a replacement." From Mrs. Canfield this request was in the nature of a plea. I told her that I would think it over.

It was Miles who helped me to my decision. Since the inquest his manner toward his mother had softened. "Mother isn't all bad, you know," he told me the weekend he and his mother came up. "This business has been a terrible shock to her. Even though she gives the appearance of calm self-sufficiency, she's really a very nervous woman. Anything that upsets her routine, her set way of thinking, makes her ill. That is one reason I had to take her away when all this first blew up ten years ago. She was on the verge of a breakdown, and it was a long time before we could get her straightened out. If you would stay, it would help her now." He had taken my hand when he spoke; his eyes were earnest and imploring. How could I refuse? I agreed to stay on for two or three weeks.

But the weeks stretched into a month, and soon there would be Christmas. The workmen came and concentrated on the white and gold room. In addition to restoring the old fireplace, they ripped up the thick white carpeting, peeled off the poppy entwined wallpaper, and refurbished the original oak paneling beneath. The windows and their ledges were trimmed with a soft green. Transformed, the room gradually lost its grim aura.

Miles and his mother came every weekend. Miles no longer spent the nights at the Inn but slept downstairs in the sunroom. I had thought that his coming up so regularly was done as a kindness to his mother, an atonement for all the years he must have unrealistically blamed her for making life so unpleasant for Arabella, causing her to run away with Morley. But one memorable night I realized that his visits had another purpose.

It was a week before Christmas. The first snow had fallen, and Miles and I sat by the leaping kitchen fire shelling walnuts. Mrs.

Canfield had gone up to bed. We were drinking sherry, as I recall, and whether it was the mellow wine or the close warmness in the kitchen, I don't know, but Miles for the first time began to talk of his past. He spoke of Arabella, how he had met and loved her, and how he had come to know soon in their marriage that she was a shallow, greedy woman. Despite that, he had continued to love her. "Maybe you would call it an obsessive infatuation. She was so beautiful and so gay when she wanted to be. At the beginning she did give me some happy moments, but she grew bored quickly. I know that now. But in those days I refused to see it. The more I showered her with gifts, the colder she seemed to grow. Every dime I made or had went for clothes and jewels, and I went on giving and giving . . . but she met Steve Morley . . ."

He paused and looked into the fire. Then, smiling ruefully, he said, "She wanted to have fun. I really don't think she was any more in love with Steve than she was with me. But all those years she was gone, I couldn't help hating him, hating her, and wanting her back. This house, that room, would reopen old scars. Sounds foolish for a grown man to behave that way. But you see, Mother had shielded me from the world so long, and Arabella was my first love, my first hurt.

"Then, when I found her, it all changed. Although it seemed a rotten way to die, even for her, it was hard to forgive her for what she did to poor Dan Tuckerman's unworldly soul. But now that's all behind me. I can forget. You might say the ghost has been exorcised."

Later we went out for a walk in the new snow. And like two children let out from school, we ran across the meadow making tracks in the pristine snow. We took to throwing snowballs and laughing. It was after one particularly big lump of snow spattered my face that Miles ran up to say he was sorry. But he took me in his arms instead and kissed me.

Never had the world looked so radiant as that miraculous moment, the stars so crystal sharp, the snow-laden trees so like shapes in a fairy tale, and the lights of Canfield House so warm and cheerful. I was reborn, someone new and wonderfully strange in a new, happy world.

As I write this now, I am Mrs. Miles Canfield. Miles and I spend our weekends and our holidays at Canfield House. Mrs. Canfield, the restoration completed, has moved there permanently. She grumbled a bit when I became Miles' bride. But when she knew that I was not likely to run off with another man and, more important, the Canfield money or silver, she came to accept me.

Miss Thornbury went abroad to Spain. I understand she is living in the English colony in Barcelona, where to be invited to her afternoon teas is a mark of social acceptance. There have been rumors that she also has a fondness for Spanish wine, but on the whole they say she's quite happy. Dolly still works at Canfield House — daily, now that Mrs. Canfield is there. She sold the grocery store after her Mr. T. was sent up to the state prison for life. Although she seldom speaks of him, I know that she visits him regularly. She is the same cheerful, kind soul, with malice toward no one.

Steve Morley got a prison term for attempted burglary — breaking and entering, I think it was, which, as Miles said, was the understatement of the year.

Damon recovered from his wound and shambles about, doing his work faithfully, if a little clumsily. The shock of Morley's bullet restored him to partial speech, but he has been a mute so long that he prefers to continue his silence.

There are still times when the sight of a red-brown elm leaf, a wet, muddy footprint, or the smell of burning cloth will serve to flash the whole terrible nightmare before me again. Sometimes, I wonder if Miles is reminded of Arabella and his ordeal by little things, too — the sight of long golden hair, a string of pearls, or a red dress. I asked him just once. He teased me so unmercifully that I flew into a rage, and we had our first quarrel.

We made it up, of course. "We're happy, aren't we?" asked Miles.

"Oh, yes," I answered.

He kissed me. "Then why look back when we have *now?*"

And he was right.